DWELLERS IN DARKNESS

Borgo Press Books by JOHN RUSSELL FEARN

1,000-Year Voyage * *Account Settled* * *Anjani the Mighty: A Lost Race Novel* (Anjani #2) * *Black Maria, M.A.: A Classic Crime Novel* (Black Maria #1) * *Bury the Hatchet* * *A Case for Brutus Lloyd* * *The Crimson Rambler: A Crime Novel* * *Death in Silhouette* (Black Maria #5) * *Don't Touch Me: A Crime Novel* * *Dynasty of the Small: Classic Science Fiction Stories* * *The Empty Coffins: A Mystery of Horror* * *The Fourth Door: A Mystery Novel* * *From Afar: A Science Fiction Mystery* * *Fugitive of Time: A Classic Science Fiction Novel* * *The G-Bomb: A Science Fiction Novel* * *The Genial Dinosaur* (Herbert the Dinosaur #2) * *The Gold of Akada: A Jungle Adventure Novel* (Anjani #1) * *Here and Now: A Science Fiction Novel* * *Into the Unknown: A Science Fiction Tale* * *Last Conflict: Classic Science Fiction Stories* * *Legacy from Sirius: A Classic Science Fiction Novel* * *The Man from Hell: Classic Science Fiction Stories* * *The Man Who Was Not: A Crime Novel* * *Manton's World: A Classic Science Fiction Novel* * *Moon Magic: A Novel of Romance* (as Elizabeth Rutland) * *The Murdered Schoolgirl: A Classic Crime Novel* (Black Maria #2) * *One Remained Seated: A Classic Crime Novel* (Black Maria #3) * *One Way Out: A Crime Novel* (with Philip Harbottle) * *Pattern of Murder: A Classic Crime Novel* * *Reflected Glory: A Dr. Castle Classic Crime Novel* * *Robbery Without Violence: Two Science Fiction Crime Stories* * *Rule of the Brains: Classic Science Fiction Stories* * *Shattering Glass: A Crime Novel* * *The Silvered Cage: A Scientific Murder Mystery* * *Slaves of Ijax: A Science Fiction Novel* * *Something from Mercury: Classic Science Fiction Stories* * *The Space Warp: A Science Fiction Novel* * *A Thing of the Past* (Herbert the Dinosaur #1) * *Thy Arm Alone: A Classic Crime Novel* (Black Maria #4) * *The Time Trap: A Science Fiction Novel* * *Valley of Pretenders* * *Vision Sinister: A Scientific Detective Thriller* * *Voice of the Conqueror: A Classic Science Fiction Novel* * *What Happened to Hammond? A Scientific Mystery* * *Within That Room!: A Classic Crime Novel* * *World Without Chance*

THE GOLDEN AMAZON SAGA

1. *World Beneath Ice* * 2. *Lord of Atlantis* * 3. *Triangle of Power* * 4. *The Amethyst City* * 5. *Daughter of the Amazon* * 6. *Quorne Returns* * 7. *The Central Intelligence* * 8. *The Cosmic Crusaders* * 9. *Parasite Planet* * 10. *World Out of Step* * 11. *The Shadow People* * 12. *Kingpin Planet* * 13. *World in Reverse* * 14. *Dwellers in Darkness* * 15. *World in Duplicate* * 16. *Lords of Creation* * 17. *Duel with Colossus* * 18. *Standstill Planet* * 19. *Ghost World* * 20. *Earth Divided* * 21. *Chameleon Planet* (with Philip Harbottle)

DWELLERS IN DARKNESS

THE GOLDEN AMAZON SAGA, BOOK FOURTEEN

JOHN RUSSELL FEARN

Edited by Philip Harbottle

THE BORGO PRESS

MMXIII

DWELLERS IN DARKNESS

FIRST BORGO PRESS EDITION

Published by Wildside Press LLC

www.wildsidebooks.com

DEDICATION

To the Memory of Sydney Bounds

CONTENTS

THE GOLDEN AMAZON
by Philip Harbottle

In 1943 British writer John Russell Fearn decided to quit writing for the American pulp science fiction magazines, and to concentrate instead on books for the English market. Within a very few years he became established as a leading novelist in several genres, not only science fiction, but also mystery and detective fiction, and westerns.

His first new SF novel, *The Golden Amazon*, was published by World's Work in April 1944. In this story, a little girl of three years of age is made the subject of an idealistic scientist's illegal glandular experiments. The scientist's dream is to end world wars by creating a woman devoid of the usual lusts and frailties of mankind, who upon reaching maturity would institute a benign scientific rule. But the apparently successful experiment has a flaw: it instills into the girl a hatred for all men, and a ruthless cruelty. Her supernatural scientific gifts enable her to master atomic power, and practically leads her to destroy the world. She breaks the will and strength of men, and elevates women to positions of wealth and power. She also discovers human synthesis, and by this means she is able to escape retribution when she is eventually overthrown. She is seen to collapse and die, a victim of consuming ketabolism, echoing the memorable finale of Rider Haggard's *She*. In actuality, it was only her synthetic image, and this paved the way for the *Golden Amazon Returns*, and further sequels

Fearn sold reprint rights in the first novel to the prestigious Canadian magazine, the Toronto *Star Weekly*. The magazine carried a special Comics Supplement, the centre section of which was a 'complete novel', published in newspaper format. Aimed at a general readership, the novels were written by the top popular novelists of the day, including John Dickson Carr, Ellery Queen, and P. G. Wodehouse. They sold hundreds of thousands of copies, and the novels were syndicated to several American newspapers in the Maine and New York areas. The Amazon novels enjoyed extraordinary popularity (especially with Canadian housewives), and ran for the next sixteen years following the appearance of the first novel in the March 3, 1945 issue, ending with Fearn's sudden death in September 1960, aged only fifty-two. His final two Amazon novels appeared posthumously.

During Fearn's lifetime, only the first six novels were published in British hardcover editions from the World's Work in England, after appearing in the *Star Weekly*. This was because the publishers discontinued their entire fiction line in 1954. However, the Amazon novels continued to appear in the *Star Weekly*, eventually notching up twenty-four titles.

Fearn had resold paperback rights to the Canadian publisher Harlequin Books, but after publishing only the first three titles, they stopped publishing SF and other genre fiction to concentrate on their famous Romances line.

Meanwhile, as early as 1949, Fearn had realized that the Amazon series had the potential to run indefinitely. This presented him with a problem, however. The 'origin story' of the Golden Amazon was conceived and actually set during the Second World War. Subsequent novels were written during the war and the immediate postwar period, and projected their stories only a few decades into the future.

He very astutely realized that to keep ahead of reality, he needed to move the Amazon *further* into the future—first into the outer solar system, and thence to the stars. So with the seventh novel, he introduced a new main character, Abna of Atlantis—someone as equally intelligent, and even stronger than herself. These dynamics provided him with an *interstellar* canvas, thus ensuring that the series would remain ahead of reality.

Fearn's strategy was a great success, and the Amazon novels retained their popularity, ending only with his tragically early death in 1960. By then he had written a further twenty Amazon novels, and made preliminary notes for his next (which would later be written by Fearn's biographer, Philip Harbottle).

Long after Fearn's death, his entire Amazon series

would eventually see print from the pioneering US small press Gryphon Books in limited paperback editions, and later by the Canadian Battered Silicon Dispatch Box small press in their hardcover Omnibus series.

This new Borgo Press paperback series will be the first trade edition of all twenty-one of these later novels by Fearn, beginning with the seventh novel in the original series. First published in 1949 as *Conquest of the Amazon*, I have edited it slightly as *World Beneath Ice* (The Golden Amazon Saga, Book One) so that it can be read and enjoyed by new readers who may be totally unfamiliar with what had gone before. Subsequent novels have also been slightly edited for modern readers.

The publishers hope that this new series may create many more "fans of the Amazon." Meanwhile, any reader interested in seeking out the earlier six Golden Amazon novels will find that they are readily available on the internet, and in numerous earlier paperback and hardcover editions.

* * * * * * *

To date, readers can enjoy the following new Borgo Press editions:

Book One: *World Beneath Ice*

In destroying the threat of an alien invasion, the Golden Amazon had inadvertently caused a decline in the sun's heat, encasing Earth in an ice sheet that threatens to eliminate humanity. The Amazon encounters Abna, a descendant of Atlantis, stronger and even more scientifically advanced than she, and the ruler of an Atlantean colony still surviving in a protected environment on Jupiter. She refuses his offer of marriage, but agrees to form an alliance in order to restore the sun and save the Earth. One thing that Abna has not told the Amazon is that all the females of his race have been wiped out by a bacilli infection....

Book Two: *Lord of Atlantis*

A gigantic ridge of land rises from the Atlantic floor, causing massive tidal waves on either side of the ocean. Even stranger, both England and America are then assailed by an invasion of prehistoric monsters! A gigantic domed city rests on the newly risen plateau, whilst out in space an alien spacecraft orbits the Earth. Such are the mysteries and challenges facing the Golden Amazon, self-appointed governess of Earth, as she struggles to unravel the maze of mystery that was the deadly legacy of Atlantis!

Book Three: *Triangle of Power*

The marriage of Violet Ray Brant—better known as The Golden Amazon—and Abna of Atlantis should have ushered in an era of peace and scientific prosperity to the people of Earth. But an unexpected turn of events finds Abna betrayed and marooned on a satellite of Jupiter, and the Amazon flung far beyond the Solar System. With Earth's two protectors removed, the planet is now at the mercy of another Atlantean, the master scientist Sefner Quorne....

Book Four: *The Amethyst City*

The metaphysical union of the Amazon and Abna results in the mental creation of a fully mature daughter— Viona. Quorne, still struggling for domination, forces Viona into a marriage ceremony, and impregnates her. But with the intervention of Tarnec Brodix, a super-mind from an external universe, Quorne and Viona are separately flung into an ultra-dimensional limbo. Abna chooses to follow after his daughter, leaving the Amazon to brood over the disaster, alone in the Amethyst City of Saturn.

Book Five: *Daughter of the Amazon*

A miscalculation by the super-mathematician Tarnec Brodix destroys his universe, and the fault spreads into the Earth universe in the form of a Dark Tide of Absolute Nothingness. Unable to save himself, Brodix transfers his knowledge into the one mind powerful enough to receive it: that if Sefian, the son who has been born to Viona and Quorne. Sefian rapidly evolves, and, no longer human, after saving the Earth universe, vanishes into the greater universe, to seek new challenges. Then the Amazon is confronted with a further puzzle—a large section of the planet Neptune is discovered to be an exact duplicate of the Earth!

Book Six: *Quorne Returns*

The bacterial intelligences of Neptune plan to conquer Earth by replacing humans in key positions with alien duplicates. The Neptunians are themselves subjugated by the sinister Atlantean scientist, Sefner Quorne. Alerted to the threat, the Golden Amazon hits back by creating the ultimate doomsday weapon—only to precipitate a reprisal from the denizens of another universe....

Book Seven: *The Central Intelligence*

The Golden Amazon's arch-enemy, Sefner Quorne, discovers that all mental gifts, such as memory and creativity, are something that is broadcast throughout the universe by a Central Intelligence—and then interpreted according to the quality of the individual brain of the recipient. At the surprising suggestion of his wife, Viona, the Amazon's daughter, Quorne travels with her to the very center of the universe, in order to wrest the secrets of mentality from the very source itself!

Book Eight: *The Cosmic Crusaders*

The Golden Amazon renounces all ties with Earth when, together with her husband, Abna, and her daughter, Viona, she sets off on a journey to explore the cosmos. On the strange worlds of Alpha Centauri, she encounters Mizanu, the embodiment of evil—a planet-sized hypertrophied brain! Its baleful, crushing mental power threatens to reach out beyond the double-system of Alpha and Proxima Centauri to engulf the Earth and all the other inhabited planets of the galaxy—unless the Amazon can destroy it first!

Book Nine: *Parasite Planet*

The Cosmic Crusaders discover a fantastic world of mental parasites drawing form and substance from our own Earth, fifty light years distant. The planet is ruled by a being identical to the Golden Amazon herself—but an Amazon who's coldly scientific and vicious, mirroring the original Amazon as she had once been early in her career. Inevitably, they become locked in a deadly duel—to the death!

Book Ten: *World Out of Step*

The Cosmic Crusaders find themselves on a planet that seems mysteriously not to conform with natural law, a world out of step with the universe. It leaps ahead into time at unexpected moments, thereby suddenly adding many years of age to the flower-like inhabitants, and killing tens of thousands of individuals through death and old age. In trying to find the alien menace responsible, The Golden Amazon and her fellow Crusaders are flung backwards and forwards through time and space, threatening their own survival....

Book Eleven: *The Shadow People*

The Cosmic Crusaders discover a planet whose people are subject to a baleful influence from outer space that sweeps across their world—and for a brief while embraces every man, woman and child. It stirs the emotions of the sexes against each other. Men desire only to destroy women, and women men. Only those with higher types of mind are able to build a resistance against it. The struggle is dire and dreadful, and leaves its victims physical and mental wrecks. The less fortunate are left dead after the Wave has passed.

But when the Crusaders identify and destroy the source of the problem, they precipitate an even greater menace....

Book Twelve: *Kingpin Planet*

The Cosmic Crusaders are plunged into a strange new space, where all the probabilities of electronic law were strangely altered, a complete and stunning inversion of the so-called natural laws. They discover the mysterious silver planet of Tuca, and deep below its surface they find an enigmatic machine—the legacy of a vanished race. Masters of science, they had overreached themselves by constructing a strange machine that could alter the very laws of nature and electronic probability. The machine had ultimately destroyed them, and blasted a neighboring planet into a cosmic cinder—and unless the Cosmic Crusaders can stop it, it may well destroy the entire universe!

Book Thirteen: *World in Reverse*

Continuing their cosmic crusade amongst the stars, the Golden Amazon and her companions discover a planet in another space where living beings are being synthetically created. The mystery deepens with the discovery that the synthetic race is evolving backwards! Determined to solve these mysteries, the Crusaders find themselves up against the Mithons, a sadistic alien race led by a being known as the Supreme One. Can the Amazon save the day?

CHAPTER ONE
FLIGHT INTO DARKNESS

Darkness, utter and complete. A darkness so intense it was more than blackness: it was the utter absence of all light. In front, to the rear, on all sides, there was not a star, not a glimmer, not even a luminous smudge— and such a condition, in the midst of the Milky Way, was rather surprising.

The only light in the Universe at the moment was inside the huge spaceship *Ultra*, moving leisurely through the vacuity. The light, atomic-powered, speared back from polished facia and switches, from banks of instruments and the complicated mass of the power plant. Everywhere inside the ship was drenched in the soft radiance, but outside lay the brittle, deadly dark of the void of space without a single guiding star.

A lone observer, clothed entirely in close-fitting black, stirred at last from before of the giant outlook windows of non-reflective glass. She rose and stretched her arm languidly—a magnificent figure of a woman, perfect in physique, beautiful of face, ageless in years. The fabulous golden Amazon of Earth.

"No end to it yet, apparently," she commented.

"Maybe it's time we had a meal, then we can look again."

"Good idea," replied the giant at the control board, and he put in the automatic pilot and then rose to his feet—a classic god of a man, standing seven feet tall and proportionately broad. Here was Abna, once lord of Jupiter, but now the husband of the Amazon and, with her, joint leader of the quartet known as the Cosmic Crusaders, At the moment the other two members of the quartet—Viona, daughter of Abna and the Amazon, and Mexone, husband of Viona, were in the sleeping quarters, waiting to be alerted if anything unusual showed itself.

But nothing did—or had. All four knew that the *Ultra* had accidentally wandered into the starless region known on Earth as the 'Coal Sack', and since then the great vessel had plunged onwards, and still onwards, into the unknown. It was the first time, in all the wanderings through space and dimensions, that any of the four had arrived in a space where light seemed nonexistent.

"Any ideas about this region we're in?" Abna asked, striding to the nearest window and peering into the vacuum.

"A few, perhaps, but I don't know how accurate they are."

The Amazon crossed to her husband's side and for a while they stood gazing together. Presently Abna's great arm stole around the Amazon's shoulder and he laughed a little.

"What?" the Amazon asked, surprise in her depth-less violet eyes.

"Oh, I was only thinking. We travel countless light-centuries, visit all manner of worlds and get lost in all sorts of dimensions, yet now we don't know where we are! A bit of a comedown for the great scientists, isn't it? Maybe we should go back to Earth and live a quiet life."

"A quiet life!" There was utter contempt in the Amazon's voice. "You know how much use we'd have for that don't you? Our purpose is to always keep going, to bring the benefits of science to—"

"To the worlds that need them," Abna finished "Yes, Vi, I know—but we're not doing that right now. We've been going for forty-eight hours at a speed about half that of light, and much though I hate to remind you, the power plant is not inexhaustible."

The Amazon gave a little start and pulled free of Abna's grip. With the lithe movements of a panther she hurried over to the power plant and surveyed it. Her brows knitted slightly.

"Not much left is there?" Abna asked, coming to her side.

The Amazon did not answer. She stared at the copper cube in the power plant's matrix—the copper from the atomic energy of which all motive power and light for the ship was derived. It had originally been nearly two feet square. Now it was shrunken to a quarter of the size.

"I'd better cut the accelerative power to zero," Abna

said. "Then we'll have just enough reserve to repel us from any foreign bodies that may show up.… We've got to have copper from somewhere, and quickly. When that's gone, we haven't a scrap."

The Amazon was about to reply when Viona and Mexone came into the control room, both of them obviously refreshed after long sleep.

"So we're still going!" Viona exclaimed, looking through the window.

"And only a thimbleful of power left," the Amazon answered her, grimly. "If this dark space doesn't present a copper-bearing planet pretty soon, we're going to be in difficulties."

The Amazon moved from the power plant, her face troubled. "If only we had a star, or something, on which to fix our attention!"

She turned to the windows again and stared out on the utter blackness. Then presently she looked around as Viona touched her on the shoulder.

"Maybe I'm wrong but—" Viona's blue eyes were anxious. "Maybe I'm wrong, but are the lights in here getting dimmer? They seem more green than they were. Normally they're blue-white."

The Amazon, Abna, and Mexone all gazed around them, then after a moment they looked at each other. They were convinced of one thing: there was nothing wrong with Viona's eyesight. The lights were changing color, altering even as they watched from green to a pale shade of yellow

"The light spectrum's altering," the Amazon said at

last "If the next apparent color is orange, then we can be pretty sure that light is sliding down the scale to extinction! But—why?"

Nobody answered her, for the simple reason that there did not seem to be an answer—not yet. And sure enough, with the passage of moments, the lights became a dull orange glow.

"Something, somewhere, is producing a spatial warp," Abna said deliberately. "That causes the normal wavelength of light to be either extended or contracted, to such an extent that light as such has no meaning to our eyes. And we're steadily flying to the source of the trouble, which is why our lights are dying. If we keep on going, we may fly beyond the center of the disturbance and find light gradually resuming...."

He stopped abruptly. The lights gradually dimmed, faded some more, and left the four in the control room like spectral presences. Then even this faded, and darkness came. Absolute. Complete. The overwhelming darkness of outer space.

Complete silence. None of the four moved, nor did they panic. Their nerves were too hardened to break down—but each one of them was sorely, desperately puzzled. They began to assess the position. Hurtling through utter blackness at half the speed of light, unable to read instruments, unable to produce light in any form, they had nothing left to rely on now but the utmost ingenuity and level-headedness.

"You there, Abna?" came the Amazon's voice presently.

"Still here," he responded. "Stay where you are and I'll come to you."

He moved, lunging into the utter darkness, and abruptly he found the Amazon next to him.

The Amazon felt Abna draw away from her, and for a while there was the sound of his movements and a sound like glass being tapped. After a while he came back to her side.

"Testing the thermometer," he explained. "Fortunately the degree numbers are raised, so I've been able to feel their outlines, and the mercury level actuates a sliding pointer which I've also been able to feel." Pause. "We were at sixty-five Fahrenheit: now we're at sixty-three. So we're already beginning to lose heat. Neither heat nor light is being conducted anywhere in the ship. From somewhere, something is being generated which causes space to fail in its function of carrying light and heat—and we're in the midst of it."

"We know the normal vibrations of light, and of space itself," the Amazon mused. "Suppose we find out, if possible, what the present spatial vibration is?"

"Not so easy in this utter dark, but I'm willing."

The Amazon moved, feeling her way around carefully. Abna did not attempt to help her: she was better left with unhampered movement. Out of the void the voices of Vionu and Mexone spoke occasionally, mainly to inquire as to what was being done.

"I'm finding out the vibration of the space outside the ship," the Amazon replied, amidst a clinking of instruments. "I obviously can't see these interior readings, so I'll have to grope my way outside and take a reading on portable equipment. It works on the raised slide method and has raised figure readings, so I'll be able to 'feel' the answer. That's better; I was having a bit of struggle getting into my spacesuit.... Back soon," she finished, and there was the sound of her shambling out of the control room to the emergency lock in the main corridor.

It seemed to the others, left in the dreadful darkness, that hours passed before the Amazon at length returned.

"I've taken a spatial reading, and judging by all normal standards it's completely haywire. That bears out your theory, Abna, that something is causing a warp. But it also suggests something else: a warp can be straightened. We know the exact figure for normal space, the figure necessary for it to carry light, heat, and so forth. We have only two chances—one, to fly on in the hope that we'll eventually draw away from this strange region: the other is to try and build the necessary equipment to straighten out the trouble, at least within the immediate vicinity of the *Ultra*."

"The last suggestion is obviously impossible," Viona remarked. "We can't do a thing with this utter darkness."

"We might feel our way to constructing some small, local neutralizer," the Amazon mused. "If we could do that, we could see our way to making a bigger one. No doubt about being able to construct the thing: we've all the necessary knowledge and machine tools."

"I think Viona is right," came the voice of Abna. "It's too complicated, Vi. Give it a while, and see what happens."

"Look!" Mexone cried suddenly. "The lights! I believe they're appearing again!"

Instantly Abna and the Amazon turned, looking upwards. They both felt a tremendous sense of relief, of gratitude even, at a dim vision of numberless dull red points glowing in the void. Without doubt they were the ceiling lights, and those of the switchboard.

Motionless, the four watched, and sure enough the colors began to reappear, in reverse order, merging from the red into orange, and then from orange into pale yellow, green, and finally the normal whiteness. At the same time gentle waves of warmth from the restored heaters began to make themselves felt.

"Well, thank heaven for that!" the Amazon exclaimed; she looked abruptly through the window. There was still nothing to be seen. Either there were no stars in the area, or else the spatial warp was still affecting them.

"Time we got some action on this," Abna said, picking up the Amazon's discarded space suit and putting it in the locker. "We shall have to go back through this dark area, evidently, so we'll be prepared for it. We'd better get busy with that neutralizer you suggested, Vi."

He turned to the control board and switched on the power, gradually increasing to maximum strength on the forward jets.

"What's the idea?" the Amazon asked.

"Slowing us down to a standstill—which will take a considerable time. We want to see what really lies in the dark area we've passed. There may be something intriguing, particularly if the dark area has been created artificially."

"While you two geniuses work out the details I'll fix a meal," Viona said. "Come on, Mexone—give me a hand."

They hurried from the control room, and after a moment Abna came and joined the Amazon where she sat at the console bench.

"This neutralization business is the least of our troubles, Vi," he said, glancing toward the power plant. "My main worry is fuel. If we don't get copper soon, we're done for. I haven't advertised the fact too much to Viona and Mexone, but I can't conceal it from you. I'm using up power with every moment we slow down, too."

"I'm aware of it, Abna. That's why I want to get the space warp sorted out. I refuse to believe that a space can exist where there are no planets or suns whatever. It isn't natural law. So, if we can only get light, we might be able to spot something worth tackling—for copper, I mean."

"I hadn't thought of that angle," Abna commented. "But surely, if there are planets anywhere around, us their gravitation would be obvious on our instruments?"

"Depends on their nearness. We may be too far

away for them to affect us, but that wouldn't prevent us seeing them."

The logic was obvious, so Abna made no further comment. Instead he pooled his scientific knowledge with the Amazon's in the creation of a machine calculated to restore exterior space to its normal condition. And it was a work that involved the most incredible intricacy, the use of computers, and hours of pondering over this or that detail. A meal came and went almost unnoticed, so absorbed were both of them in their cogitations.

Eight hours later they felt they had a reasonable instrument, which, theoretically at least, promised to do all they hoped.

"Definitely it should work," the Amazon said, seating herself with a touch of weariness.

"Definitely," Abna agreed, musing. "The one thing I foresee, however, is that the effect may he progressive, and that from the original 100-mile area there may spread an immense tide of neutralization throughout the whole area, much the same as throwing a stone into a small pond produces ripples right to the edge."

"It's possible," the Amazon admitted. "If so, all the better. We will be able to see farther, and as long as our neutralizer remains in action the effect will be maintained. At the very least we'll tie able to see 100 miles ahead of us."

"Which is not much use for observing planets," Viona remarked. "We'll only know there is one when we're 100 miles from it. And at our present velocity we'd never be able to pull up in time."

Abna glanced at her. "That presents no problem. By the time we've got this machine finished, our velocity will have slowed to nearly zero. After that as long as power holds out, we can retrace our way at a crawl, and the only real speed we'll gain is when we're in the actual gravitational pull of a planet. Since the accumulation of speed will be very gradual—at least at first—we'll have time to slow down before we actually sight the planet. But I'm gambling that the neutralization effect, once started, will expand way beyond the initial 100-mile radius. Right! Then that's settled. The next thing to do is get the neutralizer constructed, and in that we can all lend a hand."

Twelve hours...twenty-four...thirty-six. And in that time the *Ultra* had continued to lose speed. The neutralization machine was finished and required only linking to the power plant.

"I think we're ready," the Amazon said, giving the machine a final once-over. "Fortunately, it will operate through the insulation of the *Ultra*, so there'll be no need to take it outside. All right, Abna, link it up."

Abna nodded, made the necessary connections, and then stood back in satisfaction. Presently the Amazon crossed to the control board and took a grip of the special switch provided for the purpose.

"Here goes," she said. "And let's hope we get light on a dark subject!"

She closed the switch and a pilot light on the spatial machine lighted immediately, proving at least that power was flowing through as arranged. The quartet moved to the windows and gazed on to the all-too-familiar darkness. Seconds passed into minutes and there was no apparent change.

"Yet it's working," the Amazon said, frowning. "Why, then, do we not get a result?"

"Possibly because there's nothing within 100 miles that can show light," Abna responded. "I shouldn't worry about it too much. Give it time."

Turning, he crossed to the control board and with a final burst from the forward rockets he brought the vessel to a virtual standstill. He gave a troubled glance toward the power plant, then slowly eased the power into the rear rockets. When an infinitesimal but steady acceleration was registering he cut down to keep the thrust constant.

"We're going back the way we came, nearly the same route," he explained, as the others glanced at him. "We'll inevitably come to that dark area in time, but let's hope it won't be dark on this occasion. Incidentally, everything is contingent on the copper holding out—even the neutralizer machine, since it's powered from the plant. If the copper fails us, we'll have no lights, power, or anything else. In fact, it will be the finish."

The others glanced. There was little more than an orange-sized piece of copper left between the jaws of the power plant's matrix.

The hours passed. Sleeping and eating periods went by. The copper still decreased, and the blank void remained—at least until Viona, returning from a rest period, went to the window and stared outside. She was expecting the all-familiar dark, but this time there was something different. There were luminous edges on the face of infinity.

"Mother! Father! Come and look!"

Immediately the Amazon and Abna hurried to her side. Mexone, also, who had just come in, drifted across to the non-reflective glass.

"Stars and nebulae beginning to appear," the Amazon said tensely. "That can only mean one thing. Our neutralization of the spatial warp has had a progressive effect, just as you theorized, Abna. Definitely the view is becoming clearer with every moment."

This was definitely correct. In a matter of minutes, further stars had merged into view, while those already in sight had brightened in intensity. The darkness of the whole area was rapidly being dispelled.

"At this rate, there ought to be something visible in front," Abna said abruptly, and turned to the main front observation window. Then he gave a start. Directly in the path of the *Ultra*, lying some millions of miles away as yet, was the outermost planet of a six-planet system, lighted by an extremely distant green sun.

"From the look of things," the Amazon said, as she and the others joined him, "we must have passed very close to that planet straight ahead. Quite possibly it could be the main cause of the darkness. Wonder why?"

"I don't know. At the moment I'm interested in something far more vital. That green sun seems to suggest copper—and if it has a copper flame in its spectrum, then it's logical to think its planets must have it, too. Soon find out."

Glad of the chance for some activity at last, he swung the telescopic spectroscope into action and gazed at it intently. The Amazon watched also, and she caught her breath in satisfaction at the intense emerald flame that the spectroscope reproduced.

"That's copper, by all the laws we know," she said, her eyes bright. "In that case, we ought to land on that planet nearest us and see what we can find."

Throughout the journey the Amazon was continually making tests, and finally she made an announcement.

"No air whatever on that planet, which probably explains why everything is so sharp and clear. Apparently no water either. Gravity seems about the same as Earth's, which is an advantage. Sunlight, what there is of it, is about a tenth of that received on Earth. A desolate, twilight world, yet apparently rich in copper veins if my experiments are correct."

Abna nodded briefly. His whole attention now was concentrated on bringing the vessel down without mishap, and this did not prove a difficult task with no hampering atmosphere or adverse conditions. The *Ultra* finally leveled out, swept between two mighty mountain peaks, and then coasted down to one of the innumerable plateaus. A slight jerk and the journey was over.

The Amazon, Viona, and Mexone moved to the nearest window and gazed outside. They were not particularly impressed. The scene reminded them of a lunar landscape, except that in this case the rocks and plateau were utterly black instead of covered with reflective pumice dust. The sky, due to the absence of air, was, of course, completely black, and powdered with myriads of glittering stars and unfamiliar constellations, backed by the distant green sun with its mighty bars of zodiacal light shafting into the void.

"Seems our machine has worked all right," Abna remarked, glancing towards it. "We've certainly brought light back to this region, and from the look of things, it's still spreading out to the farther stars. I can imagine several astronomers on Earth in the far future—when the light from here finally reaches the solar system—scratching their heads and trying to figure out why the famous Black Coal Sack has suddenly become star-strewn again."

"The unexplained puzzle for us is why it was ever black in the first place," the Amazon responded; then with sudden activity she turned from the window. "However, first things first. We're here to find copper. Let's go."

It took them perhaps ten minutes to don their space suits, equip themselves with instruments, and then get the airlock open. The air rushed out of the *Ultra* in a singing hiss and left clogged masses of iron-hard frost around the rim of the airlock, where the vacuum of space held sway.

"Right?" came Abna's question, through his audio-phone.

Three heads nodded inside the grotesque transparent helmets. Abna clipped the safety line to all three belts, after his own, and then fastened the loose end to a projection on the airlock. By this means constant touch with the ship was possible. This done, Abna stepped out into the waste of rock and then stood surveying the merciless, star-dusted sky.

In a moment or two the Amazon had caught up with him, and his survey ceased. As usual, the Amazon was concentrated solely on one thing—in this case the finding of copper. The actual scenery—such as it was—presented no interest. With Abna at her side, and Viona and Mexone coming on behind, she went carefully forward over the plain, holding the long copper-detecting analyzer straight ahead of her and moving it from side to side with a fanlike movement. In practice, the instrument was not unlike a mine detector.

"Right!" she exclaimed suddenly in her audio-phone. "There's copper here—and judging from the racket the instrument's making, there's more than we can ever handle."

Abna checked her findings with his own instrument and then gave a nod. He motioned his enormous gloved hand to Mexone and Viona.

"We start drilling right here," he explained. "Unless I miss my guess, these rocks are actually copper themselves. If so, we can load the *Ultra* to the limit."

The four went to work immediately, a fantastic little

group under the icy stars. And Abna's guess that the rocks themselves were copper was substantiated a moment later as the shafting flame from their electronic drills reflected back from the gleaming metal, Copper in abundance, thousands of tons of it, ready for the picking up.

For nearly two hours the quartet were at work. While Abna and the Amazon dug the metal up in gleaming chunks—only the topside being dull in appearance—Viona and Mexone transported it back to the *Ultra* and set the shaping machine to work.

Automatically it shaved and modeled the rough chunks into gleaming cubes exactly the right size for the power plant's matrix.

At the end of the two hours the storage hold was well stocked with copper blocks, and the Amazon and Abna relaxed a little in their efforts and paused to survey the bleak desolation of the landscape.

"A wealthy planet as far as copper is concerned," Abna commented at length, "but absolutely useless for anything else. Wonder if life ever existed here?"

The Amazon did not answer. Abna glanced at her, and in the weak green sunlight he beheld her studying one of the instruments on her gold belt.

"Anything the matter?" he inquired.

"I don't quite know." The Amazon's voice was hesitant. "We don't feel it much through these suits of ours, Abna, but it may interest you to know that we're surrounded by a tremendous concentration of radioactivity. I just thought I'd test out the Geiger counter—

and look at what happens!"

The Amazon held forth the small Geiger counter instrument in her hand. It was clicking industriously, and continued to do so whichever way she moved it.

"Mmm, certainly pretty strong," Abna agreed, looking about him. "Wonder what the cause is?"

Together they looked around them, but beheld nothing that might account for the phenomenon; then the Amazon said;

"This instrument is extremely sensitive, don't forget. It would pick up radioactivity even if it were located on the other side of the planet. The impulses seem to be the strongest in...." She tested the instrument carefully. "In that direction," she said finally. "Due north."

"Where there's apparently nothing but flat plain. Only one thing we can do—use the *Ultra* and travel northwards to investigate. Let's be going."

CHAPTER TWO
UNEXPECTED ATTACK

The next line of action was soon made clear to Viona and Mexone, then—refueled with a new copper block, and having enough in reserve to go to the ends of infinity if need be—the *Ultra* lifted and began to pursue a leisurely course to the north, the Amazon keeping a constant check on the mysterious radioactivity with the ship's big Geiger counter. Always and unvaryingly it pointed north.

The desolate planet was, roughly speaking, about as big as Earth—which, to a ship like the *Ultra*, represented a mere hop as far as distance was concerned. Even so, for a long time there was no relief in the general monotony of plains, mountains, and chasms. The only possibility seemed to be that perhaps the source of the radioactivity was under the surface.

"It doesn't matter really if we never find it," the Amazon said at last. "I'm just curious, that's all, and while we're on the planet we might as well investigate it—"

"What's that?" Abna asked abruptly, staring through the front outlook window. "Sort of triangular thing in the distance? See it?"

It looked like a mighty triangle of green glass, leaping into full clearness as Abna switched on the forward floodlights.

Now indeed they could behold the weird object in all its glory. In some ways it looked like a gigantic emerald with absolutely smooth sides shearing away from a sword-pointed apex. As the ship came nearer it was plain that the object was buried to a great depth in the copper rocks, then sending up an emerald triangle to a height of 300 feet and more. There was absolutely no clue as to what the thing was, unless it was perhaps some long-forgotten monument to a civilization that had once existed here.

"Yet why should a monument emit powerful radio-activity?" the Amazon mused, as the *Ultra* passed over and flew away from the object. "It's something more than that, but I don't know what."

Abna shrugged. "Nothing to be gained by studying it, I fancy. Better leave it as one of the unsolved mysteries. This world is quite dead, and for myself, I prefer something more exciting. Any suggestions, anybody?"

It was Viona who answered him. She was perched on the observation seat beneath the high-power telescope.

"Head for the next world in the system, dad," she said. "You can see it there to the left. It seems to be populated. At any rate, it isn't a dead world like this one. See for yourself."

Abna took her place at the telescope and adjusted the powerful lenses until presently the fifth planet in this six-planet system leaped into acid-sharp focus. Though the planet was quite forty million miles away, every detail of its surface was brilliantly clear. Being somewhat nearer to the sun than its outermost neighbor, there was no cloudy obscurity about it.

"There seem to be cities. Have a look, Vi."

The Amazon took over from him, and while she studied the details and methodically went to work with analysis, Abna set the course of the *Ultra* away from the desolate world of copper toward the forty-million-mile distant neighbor.

"Yes, I should think your observations are right, Abna," the Amazon said at the end of her analysis. "A world worth visiting, even if its people are perhaps more accustomed to darkness than light. As to the rest of the facts—here they are. Gravity a little less than Earth's: atmosphere a little more nitrogenous. Humidity very low. Temperature around forty degrees Fahrenheit, which is not so warm, judged by Earth standards. Otherwise a fairly passable world, and one on which we shan't need space suits, anyhow."

"Good," Abna said, "Maybe when we get there we can exchange some information."

He settled himself at the controls and piled speed upon speed to make the forty-million-mile journey as rapid as possible. There was just time for a meal, and by then the fifth world was looming up in all its grandeur, the patchwork design of cities and landscape now clearly visible.

"What we're getting into we don't know," Abna said, as he swept the *Ultra* downward; then with a broad grin he added: "But then we never do."

The others did not say anything, but they instinctively felt at their weapons to be sure all was in order. Then, silent, they gazed out of the windows as the *Ultra* began to scream through the first layers of the atmosphere, dropping with ever-slackening speed towards one of the cities.

As it came nearer it revealed itself as composed of buildings of a uniform design. None was taller or shorter than its neighbor. Every one of them looked curiously like stone boxes, divided up into sections by broad streets on which no traffic seemed to be running. In general, the city was a big one, and Abna finally chose an open park-like space in which to land. Big though it was, it was only just large enough to take the *Ultra*'s immense size. Carefully he lowered the vessel down to a standstill, and then cut the power. In the silence the only sound was of the neutralizer still at work.

"Funny sort of city," Mexone commented, gazing through the window. "Makes you wonder if anybody lives here."

"Perhaps it's nothing better than a mausoleum," Abna sighed, reaching to the airlock control. "Anyhow, let's take a look—"

"There's quite a logical explanation for buildings like this," the Amazon interrupted; turning. "Don't forget that, normally, this region is in total darkness and cold. What would we do under the same conditions? Obviously use buildings without windows, and insulated from the outer conditions."

Abna nodded slowly, thinking. "Wonder what sort of people they are? There would be darkness inside and out. Perhaps a race of mole-like people, completely blind, thanks to eternal darkness—"

He stopped suddenly, his hand dropping from the airlock switch. Staring through the window, he motioned. It was a needless signal, for the others had already seen what he meant.

Emerging from one of the buildings was a file of beings, presumably men, and none of them was over four feet in height. In some ways they looked like aborigines, but a great deal more refined. In general physique they were similar to humans, with strong if short bodies, muscular arms and legs, and a great shock of black hair on their heads. The clothing was light and almost non-existent, and embellished with many curiously-fashioned jewels which possibly had the main basis in copper. As they came nearer the *Ultra* they broke up, like puzzled children, and approached the ship cautiously from various directions. Nowhere was there a weapon to be seen among them.

"Are they children or adults?" Viona asked, watching.

"Adults, I think," Abna answered her. "But obviously of a very simple type—"

"Nice olive green skin they've got," Viona added; then she gave a start. "But it may not be that color really. It's the green sun that is probably responsible.... Good heavens! Have they got eyes, or haven't they?"

"No," the Amazon said quietly. "They haven't."

That was the curious thing. As the creatures came right up to the ship and seemed to somehow be looking at it, it became quite plain that they had no eyes—only a hardly visible scar like two inch-long lines—where eyes might once have been. Nor was there anything to suggest surgical removal of the eyes: it looked as though there had never been any. Noses, mouths, and ears were all present, but only scars for eyes.

In the lead, Abna stepped out on to the park-like space with the others behind him. Immediately he did so the little people swept up to him with unerring certainty, chattering in a peculiarly musical language and gesticulating with the arms, and yet their attitude seemed generally friendly.

"What do we do?" Abna asked, glancing at the Amazon. "Follow the usual procedure and put one of them under the Education Machine? We can exchange the language thereby."

"That," one of them said—or seemed to say, "is quite unnecessary, friend. I think we can make ourselves understood."

Abna looked surprised for a moment. The one who had apparently spoken—the nearest of the party—had not moved his mouth in the slightest, and yet had made himself perfectly audible.

"Why so puzzled?" The Amazon glanced at Abna. "He's obviously a natural telepath. We've come across them before, but few of them had the art so well developed. 'Think' back at him; and see what happens.… In fact, I'll do it myself."

She concentrated for a moment, and was rewarded by a broad smile from the little being who was obviously the leader.

"I understand yon perfectly. You are the Golden Amazon of Earth, and this is Abna of Jupiter.… The others are—er—Viona, your daughter, and Mexone, her husband."

"Right," the Amazon 'thought' back. "Who are you? What kind of a world is this?"

"That is a long story, Golden Amazon, and this is not the place to tell it. For the moment I would merely say that you are very welcome guests here.… Shall we go to my quarters?"

Since the others were also receiving the mental words, the Amazon did not need to explain. She glanced at Abna.

"Might as well," he assented. "But first I'll take the usual precautions."

Turning, he depressed the exterior combination switch of the airlock and watched it ponderously close. Then he gave a nod.

"All right, we'll come with you," he 'thought.'

The little man nodded, made a brief motion to his followers to fall into line, then he led the way back toward the buildings from which he and his comrades had originally emerged The quartet followed behind him, then they stopped when inside the dwelling, the door shut, and they found themselves in complete darkness.

"I don't like this one little bit," came the voice of Viona.

From the sound of things, the little man and his comrades were marching on steadily. Their footsteps were receding into distance.

"I don't know how they do it, but they seem completely at home in the dark," Abna commented. "Fact remains that we're not, so here goes."

He yanked an atom torch from his belt and snapped it on. The brilliant beam was a relief in the blackness, and it picked up the little man and his comrades quite a distance away, marching down a long ramp into the depths of the underground.

Abna, his torch blazing, started moving swiftly. By the time he had caught up with the file, the Amazon, Viona, and Mexone also had their own torches in action, casting a blaze of brilliance on smooth, man-made walls, and ahead of them down the long and seemingly interminable ramp.

"You fell behind," came the thoughts of the little leader. "What was your trouble? Can you not find your way in darkness?"

"No," the Amazon mentally answered, bluntly. "In the dark we are helpless. I can see in normal darkness, but not the awful pitch that exists here. With these torches we're all right."

"If they give you comfort, Golden Amazon, then use them by all means. We do not need light. Extrasensory perception makes eyes unnecessary."

"Meaning?" Abna asked curiously, tramping steadily.

"Meaning that through the centuries we have developed a sense which is equivalent to sight. We sense objects instead of seeing them, and sense them so accurately that, by comparison, sight is almost slow."

He resumed the journey to the city, and in a matter of minutes it had been gained. The four passed several more men and women as they progressed, and were treated to eyeless glances of curiosity—and that was all. Until finally, by a route that seemed to take in many roads and byways, the little man and his file of followers reached a particularly large building, the doors of which were flanked on each side by more little men, all of them heavily armed. They came to attention for a moment as the party passed, and then relaxed again.

"Here are my headquarters," the little man explained, leading the way along an enormous hallway. "As you may have gathered, I am a person of some importance—no less than the acting leader of my people."

He stopped before a massive door that was obviously made of copper, then with a brief motion he dismissed his followers and opened the door wide. Still with their torches in action, the four passed into a large, comfortably furnished room and wanted for the next move.

"Be seated," the acting leader invited, motioning to low-built chairs and settees. "I will have refreshment brought."

Somewhat wearied by the long tramp they had had, the four sank down gratefully in the chairs, relaxed, and looked about them, their torches flashing up and down copper walls, and upon all manner of precious stones deeply imbedded in the metal. The chairs, too, were provided with cushions of enormous size, woven from some kind of fabric similar to cloth-of-gold. There was a wealth about this dark, strange world that was singularly surprising.

In the torch beams' reflection the little man crossed to a vast desk, pressed a button, and then waited. After a moment or two a slender, graceful woman, as blind as the rest of her race and standing about three feet six, entered. She took the leader's order and then with an obeisance she departed.

"Refreshments will not be long," came the leader's thoughts, as he drew up a chair so that he was seated in the center of the quartet. "In the meantime, perhaps I can explain a few things. I know your names, so you may as well know mine. I am called Gregor the Fourth, that is, the fourth Gregor in a line of rulers. Normally, this world of ours, and the neighbor planets around it—and far out into the void—is wrapped in total darkness and cold. For that reason we live deep under the surface, always in darkness and cold, to both of which conditions we are attuned. For centuries past our scientists have believed that the cold and dark are normal conditions—yet suddenly these two conditions ceased. Light came, and warmth as well—conditions which we have never experienced before. The warmth hasn't affected us much, since it seems we can exist in cither heat or cold, and the light means nothing because we cannot see it. We go on using our extra-sensory perception."

"Which I still don't think is equal to sight," the Amazon commented. "But then, I may be wrong, not having the power of extrasensory perception."

There was a pause for a moment as the servant arrived with the refreshment. It seemed fair enough food and drink, though oddly tasteless when the four came to try it.

"Otherwise, except for your peculiar evolution, you live a happy and—to you—normal existence?" Abna asked, perching his torch so that the beams reflected back from the ornate ceiling.

"That is so. We are a complete civilization, a brotherhood. We do not envy each other, and our life is built up in mutual trust and trade. We are not enormously advanced or avaricious, nor do we wish to be.… Whether the same applies to the inhabitants of our neighbor world, I do not know. Somehow, I rather think not."

"Neighbor world?" the Amazon asked. "Which one? We visited one before we came here, but it seemed to be deserted. The outermost planet—"

"No, not that one, Golden Amazon. I refer to the fourth planet from the sun—Dius, as we call it. It is inhabited, and by an underground race like us. But somehow they do not seem as contented as us, and in some ways are differently evolved."

The four waited for the leader to elaborate, but he did not do so. Instead, he took some of the food, ate for a while in silence, and then continued:

"Our scientists are at work now trying to discover why light and warmth came back to this region. I say 'came back,' because we assume there must once have been both, which mysteriously ceased."

"Certainly there must have once been both—or at least, light," the Amazon said, surprisingly. "And if light, then there was probably warmth, too. If you wonder why, I say that I'll explain. You and your race all have the formation of eyes, but no eyes themselves. You have the remains of seeing organs, which proves that at some time in the past the race had use of them; then, when darkness came and they were useless, Nature ceased to create them."

"Very interesting," Gregor reflected. "You have set me wondering why darkness came to this system and part of the heavens. Maybe we shall know someday.... Just as maybe we shall know why light and warmth returned."

"The answer to that is not far to seek," Abna said. "We brought back light, in order to save ourselves from disaster. I'm surprised you haven't read that from our thoughts."

"Maybe I could have done if I had made the effort, but it is not my wish to pry.... But how did you accomplish this miracle? What wonderful thing did you do?"

"Well, it's rather a matter of complicated science," Abna said evasively. "The effect is still in action aboard our spaceship, but now I'm wondering if we did the right thing in restoring light and heat to this region. Perhaps we shouldn't have."

"I think you should," Gregor said quickly. "It is obvious that light was intended in the beginning, and that the darkness is the wrong conception. Thank you, my friends, for what you have done. Maybe, thanks to your efforts, we shall be able to resume the surface of our planet and in time, who knows, future generations may be born with eyes...."

Whatever else Gregor was going to say was drowned out by a sudden colossal explosion. Not a second afterwards the reverberation of the explosion made itself felt—and the outcome was catastrophic. Even as the quartet sprang to their feet in alarm, and Gregor turned his head in alarm, the entire great room succumbed to the enormous vibrations. Walls caved inwards: the ceiling ripped in two, and a huge fissure ran the length of the floor. Instantly the four torches of the quartet were extinguished and from then on, in total darkness and overwhelming noise, they protected themselves as best they could from a hail of masonry and metal as the building simply fell to pieces.

For perhaps two minutes the upheaval lasted, then ceased as abruptly as it had begun. The Amazon, pinned down by a heavy load of fallen metal from the ceiling, stirred slowly and painfully, only to relax at the crushing weight across her legs.

"You all right?" came the anxious voice of Abna right beside her; and a second later his hands fumbled around in the dark, seized her arms, and helped her to his feet.

"I seem to be all right," she answered. "But where are Viona and Mexone?"

"I'll soon find out." Abna raised his voice: "Viona! Mexone! Where are you? Gregor—where are you?"

From Viona and Mexone there came no response, but from Gregor there was a faint mental fluttering, the thoughts of a man having a desperate struggle to remain conscious.

"Help me, please. I—I will direct you...."

Immediately the Amazon and Abna began moving, holding on to each other in the pitchy blackness, stumbling helplessly over chunks of metal and fallen masonry.

"Get me free," came Gregor's whispering thoughts. "Get me free, good friends."

It was by no means an easy job, but eventually it was accomplished. Gregor the Fourth was dragged out by Abna's mighty arms and set on his feet. Thoughts still came, so evidently he had not relapsed into unconsciousness.

"Thank you, my friends—thank you a thousand times. I feared I would die with the weight of metal pinning my chest."

"What happened?" Abna demanded. "Was it an earthquake, or what?"

"As yet I cannot say.... We have rescue work to finish. Viona and Mexone—over there. Partially buried."

'Over there' might have been anywhere so far as

the Amazon and Abna were concerned, but as Gregor began to move, they clung on to him, and he eventually led them through the darkness to yet more metal, with the unconscious Viona and Mexone buried in the midst of it.

"How badly are they hurt, Gregor?" The Amazon asked anxiously. "Tell us."

"Both have serious head wounds, as far as I can tell. The girl has a badly crushed skull and the young man seems to have a blow on the head as well as a severe blow on the chest.... The girl hardly seems to be living."

The Amazon made a desperate movement in the darkness. "Abna, what do we do to help them? If only we had a light...."

"We don't need it," he answered quietly. "Metaphysical power can supersede all lights, both for ourselves and for them. Silence, I pray you—you too, Gregor. I have mental work to do."

Gregor obeyed instantly, and because she knew the astonishing results that could be achieved by Abna's metaphysical powers, the Amazon also fell silent, and waited...and still waited, in the crushing darkness. Then presently there was a voice, weak at first and then gaining strength

"Mother! Where are you? Dad! Mexone! Can you hear me?"

"Here," Mexone replied promptly, before the Amazon could speak. "What's happened? You hurt, Viona?"

"No, I'm all right. Where are you?"

There was the sound of movement and clinking of metal—then suddenly Abna spoke.

"All right, there's nothing to worry about. The pair of you have been pretty well laid out, but you are all right now, apparently."

"For which many thanks, dad," came Viona's voice in quiet sincerity; then her tone suddenly changed. "But what's going on? What suddenly happened to wreck the place?"

"That we must discover immediately," Gregor said promptly. "Here, give me your hand, one of you, and I will lead you."

The Amazon complied and, in a long chain with Gregor in the lead, the party stumbled and slipped their way over debris, their useless eyes searching the darkness. It seemed an eternity of wandering followed, until suddenly there came the sound of many running feet and a turmoil of thoughts came tumbling into their minds as several of Gregor's people 'talked' at once.

"It was an attack, Excellency! From outer space!"

"Most of the shield to the underground is destroyed—"

"We had no chance to save ourselves—"

After which there was such a deluge of mental statements that the quartet could not sort them out. They stood waiting in the darkness, trying to figure out what it was all about; then at last Gregor started to explain.

"A most unexpected happening, my friends, and I am at a loss to understand it. It seems that suddenly, without warning, the people of our neighbor planet Dius, the fourth world from the sun, launched an overwhelming attack on us. Apparently they have created considerable damage in all parts of the planet—and for some reason the attack seems to have been concentrated on this region in particular. Why, I do not know."

CHAPTER THREE
CAPTIVES OF ARG

The journey to the exterior was a long, fumbling, and difficult job for the quartet, so intense was the blackness and so thoroughly had the invaders smashed things up—but at last, thanks to little Gregor's untiring efforts, a smudge of light began to appear in the obscurity, growing gradually into a rectangle which marked the entrance-exit at the top of the huge underground ramp. The four began to advance with fresh heart, and at last emerged into the glow of the green sun.

They turned and looked at Gregor. He was looking troubled—and with good reason. In every direction, as far as the quartet could see, there were monstrous bomb holes, smoking craters, and shattered buildings.

Finally they found the *Ultra*.

"Evidently the Diusians have considerable scientific skill in weapons," the Amazon mused, clenching her fists. "They're the first we've come across who could scorch this metal of the *Ultra*." She looked at the vacant sky with its distant green sun. "But what did they want? What was the reason for this sudden attack?"

"Something to do with the *Ultra* perhaps?" Mexone

suggested. "It is clear they've tried unsuccessfully to destroy it.... Perhaps they have watched it land here and think it a threat to their own technique of space travel."

"The idea's possible," Abna admitted, thinking. "But that does not explain the otherwise wholesale destruction of Gregor's cities. Unless it was sheer savagery...."

Abna's voice stopped suddenly. While speaking he had become gradually aware of a distant whistling sound, but had assumed it was something in the city—but now it had become really penetrating to the eardrums, and seemed to be from somewhere above.

The Amazon, Mexone and Viona all jerked their heads inquisitively skywards. So, too, did Gregor, his eyeless face turned heavenwards—and it was only a matter of seconds before he seemed to interpret the sound.

"They're coming again!" he gasped out. "Spaceships! Run!"

He did not wait to see if the quartet followed him. Instead he dived into the black eye of the underground like a rabbit darting for its burrow.

The four watched him for a moment, then looked at the sky, wincing at the appalling scream still rising with every second.

"There!" Abna said suddenly pointing. "Just coming into view!"

"Hundreds of them!" Viona gasped.

"Better take cover!" the Amazon yelled suddenly. "Inside the *Ultra!*"

She hurtled toward the ship, quickly operated the combination lock, and then raced into the ship's control room as the airlock swung wide. Not a second or two afterwards came the others, with Mexone last of all. The moment he was in, the Amazon reversed the airlock lever and snapped on the air-cylinders to bring the pressure up to normal. Then she crossed to where the others were at the windows, staring at the sky.

Almost instantly the Amazon staggered, her hands to her eyes, as a writhing mass of orange and lavender fire vomited outside the ship, shaking it with the tremendous concussion. Abna, Viona, and Mexone also reeled away, covering their faces, and then falling to their knees at the rocking of the ship.

"Who do they think they are?" the Amazon demanded furiously. "Those are small atomic bombs they're using against us."

"Obviously," Abna answered. "But why they should so concentrate on us has me beaten."

"If they think we're going to stand for this, they're vastly mistaken," she snapped. "It's about time they got a dose of their own medicine."

She did not wait for the observations of the others. Still with a glint in her eyes, she pushed over the power plant lever and then advanced the speed control to the first notch. Instantly the *Ultra* began lifting from the planet, hurtling into the sky in a long sweeping 'S.'

"Take over," the Amazon said, glancing towards Abna. "I've other things to do."

"Then you'd better do something quickly!" Viona

exclaimed, turning from the window where she was standing with Mexone. "They're coming after us like a horde of bees."

The Amazon waited, nerves taut, until the foremost ship in the line came across the cross-section in the sights. Then she pressed the button of the proton gun—by far the most destructive weapon the *Ultra* possessed. A solid wall of protons, projected on a high velocity beam, slammed into the midst of the ships and instantly reorganized—or rather disorganized—their molecular structure. There was blinding flame and soundless explosions, then at least four of the ships crumbled into great slabs of twisted, molten metal, hurtling downwards toward Gregor's patchwork world.

Time and again the Amazon blazed away with the proton gun, only to miss her targets due to the *Ultra*'s lurching. She tightened her lips, watched again, and then looked up sharply as Viona pulled furiously at her arm.

"Let's get out of here, mother! They're all using heat beams on us! Can't you feel how hot the *Ultra*'s becoming?"

"She's right," Abna said curtly, as the Amazon looked about her. "A bit more of this and those outer plates will start to melt. Once that happens we're done. We'd better make a dash for it and plow through whatever's in the way."

In the few minutes needed to reach the vessels—who formed part of the closing circle—he achieved every scrap of velocity he could manage. Burning hot, her plates glowing now in quite a few places, the *Ultra* crashed into the midst of the vessels, breaking them in pieces and sending the remains hurtling down to the world far below.

But the dash into space was not to be. The impact shattered two of the forward plates completely, already on the verge of disintegrating from the heat onslaught. With a whistling scream the air began to go.

"Seal the gap!" the Amazon shouted, struggling out of her chair for the emergency kit. "Seal it!"

There was no chance of that. The gap was too large, and the air was vanishing at lightning speed, bringing in the intense cold of the rarefied heights. In seconds the air had gone. The Amazon staggered half across the floor, then her lungs gave out and she dropped to the floor. Viona and Mexone, trying to help her, had already succumbed.

Abna made an enormous effort to slow down the *Ultra*'s velocity, but as far as he could tell, there was little effect. He collapsed to the screaming roar of tortured atmosphere as the *Ultra* flashed downwards, hopelessly out of control.

* * * * * * *

Each of the four felt, one by one, a curiously thrilling sensation through every nerve, not unlike an electric shock. For a time it produced no impression, then gradually the Amazon found herself emerging from the dark mists of unconsciousness by the very persistency of this strange vibration. Slowly she opened her eyes and looked about her.

She was in a room of some kind, the walls reaching to a tremendous height overhead and finishing in a gigantic inverted dome of deep blue glass. The walls seemed to be metal, of a curious golden color. Nowhere was there a window. Light came from an unseen source, presumably by some kind of reflection.

Puzzled, she allowed her eyes to move, then abruptly they stopped their questing. She became aware of somebody watching her. He looked very much like an Earthman in build, standing perhaps six feet, and he had nothing in common with the little beings of Gregor's planet.... Nothing in common? Yes—one thing. He had the eyeless scars on his face, but this still did not prevent the Amazon from thinking he was watching her.

He was magnificently gowned in royal purple, with very wide sleeves splashed with what looked to be gold. Probably somebody of high rank. His face was thin, austere, and not in the least friendly.

"You are better?" came his thoughts suddenly; and the Amazon gave a little start. Evidently, like Gregor and his race, he was a natural telepath, but from the clearness of the thought-message he seemed to have a much firmer grasp of the mental technicalities than Gregor.

"Yes, I am better," the Amazon thought back. "In fact, quite recovered. What happened?"

"Your vessel was saved from crashing—for two reasons. One, because we wish to study it; and two, we wish to question you and your colleagues. We brought your ship, and you, to our own world."

The Amazon studied the eyeless, coldly impartial face.

"Which is another way of saying we are captives?"

"Certainly you are captives. When we have learned what we wish to know, we shall kill you."

The Amazon straightened up and then slid from the stone block where she lay. She felt at her weapon and instrument belt, and caught her breath sharply. The belt had gone.

"Naturally," came the thoughts of the austere one, "we have relieved you and your comrades of weapons."

The Amazon kept silent, at the same time making her thoughts as blank as possible before the rapier probing of this mental expert. Turning, she looked at Abna, Viona, and Mexone. They, too, were slowly recovering now, and in a few moments had completely regained consciousness.

"One or other of you," the man said, as Viona and Mexone also came around to join the Amazon and Abna, "is responsible for violent changes on our world and system. We mean to find out the facts, and then destroy you."

"So you said before," the Amazon commented. "Don't get too sure of yourself, my friend. We are not exactly helpless."

The being smiled thinly. "I am aware that you are clever scientists, but not quite so clever as us, I think. I cannot read from your minds whence you come, but for light years around this system my name in particular is well known—and revered, even if in terror. I am Arg."

"Which, to us, doesn't mean anything," Abna 'thought'.

"I detect a cynicism in your thoughts, Abna. I would advise you to guard against it in future."

"What planet is this? Dius?" the Amazon questioned.

"Maybe that is your name for it. We name it Fond. It is the fourth planet from the primary." Pause. "Or perhaps the people of the fifth world, the Norians, call our world Dius?"

"Would the Norians be ruled by Gregor the Fourth?" Abna asked. At that the head of the other, partially bald, nodded.

"That is so. I have at times had trade dealings with that little fool Gregor, and his uneducated, unscientific people. Has he not mentioned my name to you?"

"No," Abna replied, "but he did speak of trade dealings and your ability to travel space. Certainly he did not refer to you with any emotions of fear."

"That is perhaps understandable. As yet we have not brought the fifth planet under control. We have more difficult worlds to deal with first."

"What do you want with us?" the Amazon demanded. "We are not of the fifth planet, nor of any of the worlds about here—"

"I realize that. It does not matter particularly where you are from. You constitute a very real danger to us, and I'll show you why. Come with me!"

The quartet obeyed because they were in no position to do otherwise. They followed Arg out of the forbidding-looking chamber and into a room redundant with scientific instruments. Here there were several men, not unlike Arg but not so lavishly attired, operating various machines with a remarkable blind accuracy. Taking no notice of them, Arg went to an apparatus that was obviously built on the television principle and switched it on, then he imperiously motioned for the quartet to watch the screen.

They did so, after a grim glance at each other, and presently there appeared on a screen a vision of what seemed to be a long hospital ward, lighted as usual by the mysterious indirect illumination. Changing the focus length, Arg gave a nearer view—a traveling shot, in fact—of eyeless men and women lying in earthly looking beds, practically all of them in the grip of some horrible and obviously painful skin disease. It looked like eczema in its worst form. Dozens of these hapless creatures appeared in the screen, until finally Arg cut the instrument off.

"You observe?" came his thoughts. "You are satisfied with your handiwork?"

"Our handiwork?" the Amazon repeated. "What brought you to that conclusion?"

"It requires no deduction, Golden Amazon. Before you and your comrades came into our system, and to the world of Fond, all was well with us. We progressed happily and without disease in a world of darkness and cold. With the coming of light and heat, certain of our spatial vibrations changed, most noticeably the infra-red from our sun. The result was as you have seen—deadly skin disease ending in death. Thousands have died, and thousands more will die. Because of you! You, for some reason, saw fit to bring light into our system. Light! The most deadly of all radiations to us. Not so much light itself, but all the other waves moving at the same speed and through the same medium of space. What right had you to do this?"

Abna said: "There are one or two things that need answering. For instance, though Gregor's race is similar to yours, though neither as big physically or as clever scientifically, no objection was raised at the restoration of light, and no disease was produced. How do you account for that?"

"Simple. Gregor and his race are less refined than us and not as susceptible to change. Further, the fifth planet is farther from the sun than us, and therefore not in such danger from his radiations."

The Amazon 'said': "You spoke a little while ago of the 'restoration' of light and heat, Arg. That would suggest that once it was a normal condition, but some-thing neutralized it. Is that correct?"

"Tens of thousands of years ago light and heat and other radiations were natural to this system," Arg admitted. "Then they ceased and we began to evolve in a different way, with extrasensory perception to take the place of sight, and increased internal energy to take the place of exterior warmth. Everything was organized to suit dwellers in darkness—then suddenly the former conditions are restored, with devastating results. Imagine your world, accustomed to light, suddenly plunged into total darkness. So it is with us, in reverse."

"Light is natural and darkness is not," Abna said quietly. "That is why we restored it. Whatever attributes you may have developed to counteract cold and darkness, they are not normal ones, therefore we—"

"To us they *are* normal!" Arg interrupted, harshly. "And we intend to have them back—and quickly. Now, which of you is prepared to explain how you forced space to perform its normal function—and so endangered us?"

As there was no answer, Arg finally carne to a decision. He called to two of his laboratory workers—by thought waves—and they came immediately. Then Arg continued:

"Take the younger woman to the electronic terminator and make her talk," he ordered. "Inform me when she is too weak to resist."

The two men turned promptly and seized Viona's arms. She made an unsuccessful effort to pull free. The men were far stronger than they looked, even to her tremendous strength. They forced her irresistibly away—but not for long. Without warning, the Amazon suddenly leaped, swung the nearest man around with her left hand, then smashed her right fist into the unprotected face.

The remaining man stared for a moment in sheer amazement, and it was that hesitation that proved his undoing. In a flash, regardless of consequences, aware only that her daughter was about to be taken from her and tortured, the Amazon was upon him, crushing him to the floor by main strength.

All this tremendous activity on the Amazon's part occupied only a matter of seconds, seconds in which Arg also recovered from his astonishment and signaled to the other laboratory workers to come into action.

Abna saw that signal; in consequence Arg was flat on his back a moment later, a knee in his spine and mighty arms forcing his chin and head upward and backward. Arg struggled, his thoughts a turmoil of chaotic fear. To escape from the clutch of the giant pinning him down was obviously hopeless—yet if he did not act fast, his neck or spine would inevitably break.

"Let me deal with him," the Amazon ordered. "I want to find out where the *Ultra* is."

"Okay, but he's dangerous.... Take him. He's all yours."

Abna released his hold, knowing quite well that the Amazon was well able to take care of the situation, and turned his attention to the furiously battling Viona and Mexone. It was well he did. With eight laboratory workers to fight—which seemed, with the remaining two who had tried to seize Viona, the entire staff—the younger ones were having all their work cut out. But the instant Abna lent his assistance, with his enormous size and strength, the tide began to turn.

As for the Amazon, she did not show any interest in the battle proceeding around her. Her whole attention was concentrated on Arg. From the grip of one captor, he had fallen into the hands of another—and one much more ferocious, it seemed. With twists of her arm the Amazon had him on his back, and there he remained, unable to break the grip she had upon him. "Where is our spaceship?" she asked. "You brought it to this world, you say, so where is it?"

In the brief interval that followed, Viona dealt with her most persistent attacker. A perfectly timed left uppercut took him under the chin, lifted him from his feet, and crashed him motionless to his back two yards away.

"Nice work," the Amazon said, glancing up but never relaxing her hold. "We'll make a fighter of you yet, Viona— Come, Arg, I asked you a question! Answer me!"

With her free hand she slapped the master of Dius back and forth across the face. He gasped at the sharp pain, then jumbled thoughts began to

"Your—your ship...is on the surface."

The Amazon whipped her fingers from Arg's neck and got a swift arm lock on him. She yanked him to his feet.

"You're taking us to it, Arg—and if you make one wrong move I'll kill you! That's fair warning! Now, have the rest of these men leave us alone."

Arg turned as well as he could to give the order, but there was no necessity. Abna, Mexone, and Viona, disheveled but triumphant; were just at the end of dealing with the opposition. The result of their labors lay scattered about the laboratory floor, some unconscious and others dead. With the staff thus disposed of, the laboratory was empty of workers.

"Move," the Amazon ordered, giving Arg a twitch that nearly brought him to his knees. "You chose rough methods, Arg, so you can't blame us if we repay you in the same coin."

Completely helpless, the formerly arrogant ruler was compelled to obey orders—even to the extent of telling those of his race who would have aided him to keep away. Thuswise the quartet had a trouble-free retreat from the laboratory, and afterwards along the various passages and tunnels, which from the inclination of their floors, plainly led to the surface. This was proved when at last a huge door of metal loomed before them, apparently in a wall of rock.

"Open it!" the Amazon commanded, as Arg paused. Then as he still remained inactive, she jerked him savagely. "I said open it!"

"Give me time, Amazon! The lock is controlled by thought-waves."

The Amazon waited, not at all patiently while Arg hurled his thoughts at the door. After an interval of perhaps twenty seconds the ponderous mass began to move to one side and a daylight view of the planet's exterior came into view. In another moment the five were outside, the brilliant green sun high above them.

The Amazon looked about her, still holding on to the ruler. They had emerged from the face of a cliff, which directly faced what appeared to be pastureland, and in the midst of this pastureland, apparently unharmed, was the *Ultra*. Arg's city was deep underground, with the cliff-door as one of the entrances thereto.

Arg, released, watched them walk to the *Ultra*, a quarter of a mile distant, then he turned and went back to the door in the cliff face. It opened under the usual thought influence, and then closed again as Arg passed beyond it.

"Think we've done with that fellow?" Abna asked, as they paused to survey the spaceship.

"Anything but, I imagine—but there's a chance that when we do see him again we may have things on a different footing. I'll tell you what I mean later. Right now we've work to do."

Of that there was no doubt. The front of the *Ultra* was a ruin, two of its great plates a broken mass of formerly molten metal, while the rest of the ship was scarred with the blue-black lines that told of tremendous heat.

"They must have some kind of weapon which makes good use of the restored spatial vibration," Abna reflected. "Somehow they produce a furious heat... way beyond anything we can do."

"True enough," the Amazon admitted. "But it doesn't have to be heat: it simply assumes that form. It's some kind of near-disintegration device that relies on the presence of normally functioning space to make it operate. That suggests the weapon is a new one, since space was only restored to normal when we came along.... Ever stop to think what frightful devastation they can produce on Gregor's world if they really set about it? We've got to get back to his planet and protect him and his race against any such attack— if we can. One sure way of stopping the trouble would be to let the darkness return. Their weapon wouldn't work then.… However, first things first. Let's get the ship repaired before Arg thinks of something bright to stop us."

The job done, the four returned to the control room, brought the air pressure up to normal, then quickly rose into the dark void of space. It was when they were nearly a million miles from Dius that the Amazon started to explain. She put the automatic control in position and then turned to where the others were in the act of preparing a much-needed meal.

"Did it ever occur to you," she said slowly, "that Arg is being forced to conquest by forces outside himself?"

"What are you driving at, mother?" Viona asked.

"This! While I was probing Arg's mind just before we departed, I caught a glimpse of the real man, and I'll swear he isn't any worse or any better than most of us. Almost immediately this glimpse was swamped by the arrogant front Arg normally presents—the kind of front we encountered. At the same time, curiously enough, I caught a vision of that gigantic emerald we encountered on the first planet we visited here."

"That radioactive chunk of green glass, or what-ever it was?" Mexone asked. "When we descended for copper?"

"The same. Why that thing should be mixed up in

Arg's thoughts isn't at all clear to me—so I'll make a guess. Arg and his people are probably not conquerors in the ordinary way: they're forced into it by some kind of stimulus that comes from the Emerald. Crazy, perhaps, but we've known crazier set-ups."

"Then," Abna said, pondering, "why doesn't it affect Gregor and his race?"

"I think it does, but they're not so sensitive that it makes an impression. If my guess is right," the Amazon went on grimly, "something has to be done, because driven by a mysterious stimulus like that, Arg's race may develop into a real danger with the passage of time. If the driving urge is there, they'll go on conquering—and with considerable success, no doubt, because they're no mean scientists. To defeat that possibility and restore them to normalcy, we've got to find the reason for the emerald, and if possible discover who put it there and what they're driving at."

"A pretty tall order," Viona exclaimed. "How do you propose doing it?"

"There's only one way. Explore a field that, to us, is comparatively new—Time! I suggest returning to Gregor's planet, enlisting the aid of his various workers, and building a Time mechanism in his laboratory, one capable of moving us backwards to the first cause, to the period before this System even came into being!"

CHAPTER FOUR
FLIGHT TO THE PAST

Accustomed though the others were to the Amazon's unbridled imagination and scientific skill, this latest project she had suggested caught them on the hop for the moment. They all stared rather blankly.

"All right," Abna said at length, as they settled for a meal. "All right, we're going to travel in Time for a change. What basis are you going to work off, Vi?"

"The usual one—as we did once before. We accept the proposition that it is impossible to travel in space without traveling in Time: the two are interlocked, and yet both are distinct dimensions, a dimension of space and a dimension of time. Whatever we do, whatever mathematics we may postulate, we cannot avoid the fact that we have to travel in space in a certain amount of Time. The two are utterly indispensable. But we have one advantage—the dimension of Time is circular, even as the Universe itself is circular. In the normal way we travel, as does the Universe, gradually along the circle, performing all our actions in a certain amount of space, and yet constantly drifting further into what we call the future. We can stop and ask ourselves why we do that."

"And the answer is what?" Viona asked.

"We do it because every electron and molecule in our bodies is geared to the time-ratio. All move along at the same pace. But we can alter the pace and ratio with our knowledge of electronic science. We cannot only gear our bodies to move forward far faster than normal—and therefore come to the future far ahead of what would normally be the case—but we can also so reverse the ratio that we lose ground, as it were, and therefore travel backwards into the past. We're never out of the Time-circle, though, whether moving backwards or forwards. We still are in Time, and in space."

"Summed up briefly, we're like clocks?" Abna reflected. "A clock will register fast or slow time by altering the regulator. It has not affected Time itself: only from the aspect of the clock itself. And in an extreme case a clock can be made to go backwards. As I have said, Time itself still is not affected by the fact; only from the viewpoint of the clock."

"Exactly," the Amazon assented. "That is the process in plain words—about the most unsatisfactory medium possible for explaining what is pure abstract mathematics. In figures and equations we can work it out definitely from the basic premise that past and future do not really exist, but are theoretical. Actually, there is only Now. The future has yet to come; the past has gone. We only live at the second of existence that has just come into being—and that is Now.... Our job will be to convert the electrons and molecules of ourselves and the *Ultra*, since it is in the *Ultra* that we shall travel back in Time."

"The sooner we begin, the better," Abna said, "but what happens to the nneutralizer?" He glanced towards it, still flawlessly in operation. "When we start monkeying around with Time, it will no longer function properly, will it? Everything in the *Ultra* will be affected—that included."

"We'll build another one," the Amazon said. "Gregor can have it and stay in charge of it, and this other one we'll take with us. We'll have to take it with us, for the simple reason that we want to see what's happening. Without it we'll...." The Amazon stopped and then gave a rather rueful laugh. "I'm forgetting!" she went on. "The paradoxes that pile up when one is dealing with Time. We'll let Gregor have this one. We shan't need it, because in going backwards we'll cover the Time where light exists, and then come to the point where the neutralizer is no longer in action. We shan't be able to alter anything because we cannot alter Time—only travel in it. So this neutralizer will be of no use to us."

"Which raises a point," Mexone said worriedly. "The darkness seems to have lasted for thousands and thousands of years. We're not likely to enjoy plowing through ages of dark iciness."

The Amazon smiled. "I agree—but we have the saving grace of being able to speed up our travel, so that 1,000 years of normal Time can pass in, say, ten minutes. I believe that we must finally come to a point where light exists again as a normal thing. Then we may find the reason for the emerald, for Arg's grim ambitions—for lots of things. Now, Abna, if you've finished your meal, we might as well do the preliminary calculations."

With a nod he got to his feet and then crossed over to the big computer bench where all the navigational calculations were made. Settling himself at the nearest console stool, he commenced figuring, a task in which he was presently joined by the Amazon. In silence they worked, the bright overhead light catching the gleaming golden waves of their hair. And, in equal silence, for fear of disturbing them, Mexone and Viona busied themselves elsewhere.

Ever and again the Amazon and Abna checked their calculations by means of the vessel's master computer brain, and usually found that the conclusions they had arrived at were correct. So, by degrees, and the intervention of several meals and sleeping times, the two managed to hammer out their plan. When eventually Gregor's world was filling all the void before them, they had every detail complete.

"The rest," the Amazon said in satisfaction, "is up to Gregor and his followers. I don't think we shall have any difficulty in providing materials. What we haven't got we can very soon make."

Abna nodded agreement, and there, for the time being, the matter ended. Everything now had to be concentrated on a safe landing on Gregor's world, and no distraction could be permitted.

Abna brought the vessel down gently and the people below, aware of its ponderous mass, commenced to run in all directions. By the time a landing had been made, in a narrow space between two blocks of buildings, the news had evidently been transmitted to Gregor himself for he was outside the vessel, his small friendly face wreathed in smiles. Several more of his race were at a distance, evidently none too certain of his reassurances that this was not an attack.

Quickly Abna opened the airlock and then stepped outside, raising his hand in greeting. Immediately Gregor came forward, his thoughts chiefly those of excitement. In that moment Abna had the chance to realize how much less clearly Gregor's thought-waves penetrated, compared to Arg's.

"You have returned, my friends!" the little ruler exclaimed. "I had begun to fear you had departed on some other mission and forgotten all about us—or else had been killed."

"Neither," Abna responded. "We have had an uncomfortable time at the hands of Arg of Dius, but we managed to defeat him. Many things have happened. Come into the control room and let us explain."

The little ruler promptly accepted the invitation, settled in a seat, and then listened to the thoughts of Abna and the Amazon as they explained what had been happening.

"So Arg plans the destruction of this world, too—the subjection of my people to his rule," Gregor's thoughts mused. "I can prepare for battle...."

"And you believe you can hold out against him?" the Amazon asked rather dryly, at which a rueful aspect came into Gregor's thoughts.

"No, Golden Amazon, I'm afraid we cannot. Even now Arg has produced terrific damage on our world—even though his attack was aimed primarily at you and not at us. When he really descends to destroy us, I'm afraid his superior scientific knowledge and armament will crush us completely."

"With us on your side, which we certainly shall be, he won't find conquest an easy matter," the Amazon said. "But there is just a chance that such an invasion will never come. Arg does not really want it, nor do his race. All of them, Arg included, are at the mercy of a power stronger than themselves."

"What power?" Gregor asked in surprise.

"That is a matter which doesn't concern you, Gregor, even if you could understand it, which I doubt. What we are concerned with is to help Arg out of his hypnotized state into a condition of normalcy, and save you and an untold number of worlds from future danger. When we depart from this system we want to leave you as good neighbors, with no threats of destruction from anybody. That we can do—with your help."

"Name it!" Gregor said promptly.

The Amazon continued: "We propose to travel in Time—return to the past—and find the reason for Arg's urge to dominate. We know how we can do this, but we shall need special equipment. Also, while we are gone, there is something you must do. As we told you, there is light in this system because we invented a machine called the spatial neutralizer. We are going to hand it into your keeping, from the *Ultra*, and it will be your duty to see that it is kept going. It will function automatically, but there are certain replenishments to be made to it. That will be explained in detail to you."

"Whatever you wish, my friends, shall be done."

"Secondly," the Amazon resumed, "we shall need a labor force of the best scientific experts in your race to help us build a Time-unit, which is to be incorporated inside the *Ultra*. If we do it ourselves, it will take a long time, and speed is the main thing at the moment. The designs are ready: we merely need the workers to assist us."

"And you shall have them. Where do you intend to work—here or in one of my laboratories?"

"We'll assemble the instrument in your laboratory, and then fix it in the *Ultra* here afterwards. First thing we must do is get this spatial neutralizer transferred to a place of safety, and we'll need two reliable scientists to keep watch over it in turns."

* * * * * * *

In approximately four Earth weeks the Time-unit was complete and the time had come for a test.

The Amazon stood in for the experiment, and to the watchers she seemed to fade away.

For the Amazon the effect was exactly as she had foreseen. The instant the main switch was turned on, the laboratory and the spectators started to weave fantastic patterns. While the laboratory remained unchanged, the people in it went back and forth at lightning speed as the preceding days flashed by.

Quietly and calmly she analyzed her physical reactions to the movement through Time, and discovered no ill-effects. Naturally the air pressure and supply were normal, since there had been no change in atmospheric content over the years.

Then the mechanism and the kaleidoscope of past time abruptly reversed. Things flashed back into normal and, to the Amazon, the laboratory slowly began to merge into being again. The hum of power from the machine ceased. The Amazon became aware of the expectant faces turned toward her.

"Everything is satisfactory," she announced, stepping forward; then to Abna she added: "Our calculations were correct. I went right back to the time when this laboratory was built. When we have infinite extension, we'll be able to go as far back as we wish. Only thing now is to get the apparatus aboard the *Ultra*."

Which presented no difficulty. Within an hour the instrument had been safely transported to the *Ultra*'s control room and was securely bolted to the floor, in the same place where the neutralizer had stood. The job done, the Amazon looked at Gregor and the scientists as they stood, like curious dwarfs, in the airlock.

"Is this departure, my friends?" Gregor asked, plainly disappointed; and the Amazon nodded.

"I'm afraid it has to be, Gregor—but not permanently. When we have discovered what we wish to know, we shall return. Remember that our sole object is to make this system a peaceable one, and release from slavery those who have already been crushed. Our endeavor is to save Arg from himself.... How long we'll be away we don't know. In the meantime, never relax the spatial neutralizer. Arg perhaps will hold his hand against you, thinking we are here to aid you.... That is all. Farewell for now, my friends."

Gregor gave a little obeisance, motioned to his followers, and then retired to the exterior. Abna depressed the airlock switch and then set the *Ultra* climbing rapidly—through the atmosphere and into the void of space. When he was 500,000 miles from Gregor's world he began to decelerate.

"Why stop here?" the Amazon asked in surprise.

"We don't want to influence Gregor's world when we turn backwards into time. But I think this is far enough."

"It is not Gregor's world that we wish to study—but the outermost one where the giant emerald is. That was what I glimpsed from Arg's mind as the source of his thirst for conquest. Head for an orbit about 500,000 miles from the outermost planet."

Abna nodded, and began to increase the acceleration again. The world of Gregor dropped away with ever-increasing speed, and the glittering point of the outermost planet began to assume very gradual formation. Soundlessly, with terrific velocity—but by no means the maximum speed—the *Ultra* hurtled onwards.

In three hours the distance had been covered. The

craggy, barren wilderness of the outermost planet loomed ahead, the stars reaching to its airless horizon. Gradually the *Ultra* slowed down, and slowed down still more, falling into an orbit at the required half-million miles from the planet's surface.

"I can just see that emerald object," the Amazon said, raising her head from the telescope. "Now let's see if we can find out how it got there.... Right, Abna! The Time apparatus!"

He switched it on, and after the usual delayed action the full surge of power began to work.

"We're moving back along the time track all right," the Amazon murmured tensely. "Let's hope we—"

She stopped suddenly, completely stunned by the fact that the fixed stars had suddenly ceased to be visible. Within seconds the farthermost nebulae also vanished, and then the more distant planets of the system.

"What's happening?" Viona asked in alarm. "Why's everything vanishing in this—this dark tide?"

"Fairly simple explanation," Abna said. "The time apparatus is working perfectly. We've come to the period when we started to neutralize the darkness of this region. Remember that light flowed outwards from us in a flowing tide—progressively? Well now, as we go further back in time, darkness flows in from the outside. Our light neutralization in reverse. Soon we shall be in the time before neutralization took place."

He was right. In little more than a few minutes every spot of light, including the green sun, had vanished outside. Then the lights within the *Ultra* also dimmed and expired. A blackness, almost on a par with that which they had first experienced—descended.... The Amazon's voice came out of it.

"We're back where we were when we first got here. The ship itself being in the backwardly flowing track, we are naturally absorbed into those events. But how long will it last, I wonder?"

"A long time, I'm afraid," Abna answered seriously. "Even at our present rate of fifty years to the minute of normal Time, we've got to plow through many generations at least.... All depends on whether we can stand it."

"Of course we can stand it!" the Amazon exclaimed sharply. "Why shouldn't we? We can get used to the darkness—and if we can't, we can reverse the Time-switch and go back to the light."

"I wasn't thinking entirely of the darkness. There's heat, too, remember. From this moment onwards it is no longer being conducted. Things will get colder and colder."

"There's an answer to that, too," came the voice of Viona. "If things get too bad, we can get in space suits and hope that our natural warmth will be sufficiently insulated and unable to dissipate to keep us alive. We've started on this job, and we must see it through somehow."

Nothing. Utter nothing. The time passed.

"We'd better have a meal," Abna said, and in a clumsy movement began toward the execution thereof.

At the end of the meal there was still the darkness.

Even after the sleeping period it was still there—a blackness, worse than any blindness, since all of them were in the same predicament.

"I don't know how much longer I'm going to be able to stand this," came Viona's voice. "I never thought it could be such a strain. Father, how much longer do you suppose it's going to be? It's becoming dreadfully cold, too."

"We've been traveling Time for something like fourteen hours," the Amazon said, feeling the raised numbers of the chronometer. "Fifty years a minute, that means we've gone back some—er—" She did some swift mental arithmetic. "Some 42,000 years. Not nearly long enough for the entire evolution of a race—and it must have been an entire evolution, other-wise the race would not have vestigial remains of eyes. I'm afraid we've some time to go yet."

It was close on a million years, according to the Amazon's calculations, when at last much longed for light began to return. First in the shape of nebulous smudges, then rapidly progressing to stars and planets. The green sun, much more powerful, blazed forth.... Eagerly the quartet hurried to the observation window and surveyed in surprise the same system they had formerly seen, except that in the interval the planets had altered their original positions.

"Well, now, where are we?" Viona asked, taking off her space suit and then luxuriating in the warmth around her from the heating system. "What have we discovered?"

"That remains to be seen." The Amazon was studying the instruments. "We've come nearly a million years in time—to the period before darkness descended on this region. Let's see how the outermost planet is faring."

This was no longer a planet of vast plains and inimical mountains, airless and dead, but a world of clouds, cities, oceans, and landscapes. A flourishing world, and from appearances, one at the zenith of its career.

Abna said: "The best thing we can do is go down there and—"

"It is not our wish that you should go down there, my friends!"

The voice was quiet, but it had the cold ring of absolute authority. Astounded, the quartet swung around, and stared at the unbelievable. Standing a few yards from them, having somehow entered through the *Ultra*'s invincible walls, was an immensely tall and regal being. Possibly he was eight or nine feet tall, with proportionately broad shoulders. He wore a single garment of royal purple with a slash of vivid scarlet across his chest. Otherwise his appearance was almost Earthly in general outline. An enormous forehead, hooked nose, and arrogant mouth. The hair was white, swept back in thick waves from the great brow. The general impression was one of immense power, and not a little hostility.

"Greetings," Abna said, while he tried to get the situation in focus.

"That is not meant with feeling," the being commented. "You say it while you assess the position, while you try to discover who I am and how I got here. Do not waste your time, Abna of Jupiter. You do not gaze upon the real entity, merely upon a projection of that entity's thoughts."

None of the four ventured any comment. They were feeling dwarfed and insignificant before the enormous size of their mysterious visitor.

"I have inspected each of you in detail," the being resumed. "I know the workings of every one of your external and internal organs, and you are definitely extremely low in the scale of evolution, yet imagine yourselves highly developed. Highly developed!" And there followed something that could have been a sinister chuckle.

"Are we to understand that you are a thought projection?" the Amazon asked, her voice quiet even though her temper was rising.

"I am. In my real self I live on this solitary outermost planet, engaged in scientific pursuits, which I do not wish disturbed or investigated. I saw your machine— your childish *Ultra*—and decided to project myself to warn you. Go! Leave this system and this region, and never come back. If you do, I shall instantly transform the four of you into cosmic dust."

"You seem," Abna remarked, "to have quite a marked opinion pf your own abilities!"

"With reason, Abna of Jupiter. I have the complete mastery of mind over matter. Some have it partially; others struggle for it—such as you with your puerile metaphysics—but I have it entirely. If that were not so,

I could not have boarded this vessel."

"True," Abna admitted, conscious of the fact that here, for the first time in many wanderings, was a specimen with absolute control of material forces. "Just the same, I cannot see why that should make it necessary for us to meet as enemies."

"Everybody who does not measure up to my standard of excellence is an enemy! You came to pry, to study my world. You evolved a clumsy Time-traveling method by which to do it—and it has all been for nothing. I have warned you to go! Now!'""

The four did not move. At which the apparition shrugged and seemed to smile icily. A second later a steel wall sprang into being in the center of the control room and began to move toward the four, impelled by no visible force.

CHAPTER FIVE
THE MASTER-MIND

Abruptly the moving wall vanished and gave place to an Earth woman who was somehow familiar. The Amazon started as she stared at her: it was her own mother, Irene Grayson! Then, just as quickly, the living image of Irene Grayson had given place to Chris Wilson, Ruth Dodd, and Commander Kerrigan, all people who had once featured in the Amazon's earlier life. The climax came when Dr. Axton, whose experiments had created the Golden Amazon, flashed into being for a moment and was gone.

The apparition vanished, and for a moment or two there was an aching pause. Then suddenly all four simultaneously felt a straining at their muscles and nerves, so intense it forced them gradually to their knees, mightily though they fought against it. Even as they went down the voice of the now invisible apparition spoke again.

"It would seem that you require a practical demonstration of annihilation, my friends, therefore you shall have it. By mind alone I intend to disintegrate you into dust. You and your ship...."

The frightful invisible pressure increased. Gasping for breath, nearly purple in the face with strain, the four fought with all their strength—not physically but mentally, all of them in the merciless grip of an intellectual monster who knew no pity and had no time for anything except his own power. Even Abna, expert metaphysician though he was, sank slowly down on the floor, beating his great fists against the metal plates in a frenzy of opposing, mental concentration.

To each of the four there was given the most grinding torture they had ever known, something far more subtle and inescapable than the greatest physical anguish—this attempt to tear every atom of their beings into pieces by mental power alone. Then, as they felt they could not any longer withstand the excruciating pain, the pressure suddenly ceased.

It was unbelievable—as unbelievable as the glorious sense of comfort and peace that descended when the torture ceased. Then out of this haze of drowsy well-being the voice of the apparition spoke again.

"I confess myself astounded! Never in all my experience have I known matter to be so resistant! Though I tried every mental combination, I still could not break you down. Indeed I have suffered a change of heart. You are interesting specimens."

There was a silence. During it, the quartet got up slowly from the control room floor and waited for the next.

"I have decided," the apparition announced presently. "I shall let you into the secrets you wish to know.

The purpose of your visit is to find what brought the darkness, and the eyeless people of the future. And above all the reason for the radioactive stone.... The object you mentally call the Emerald. Those things I shall reveal to you. Immediately."

And abruptly the control room of the *Ultra* was no longer there—nor any part of the ship. The four experienced a brief wave of dizziness, which set them staggering, then the surroundings were entirely changed. By some process of amazing thought-control they were transported. In silent wonder they looked about them.

They were in a gigantic room, some kind of laboratory if the various strange machines in all directions were any guide. In the midst of them, at a central desk completely covered in switches and panels, sat a small, solitary figure with a huge forehead and extremely twinkling eyes. It was not the twinkle of humor, but of vast intelligence and egotism.

"Don't stand there, my friends. Come forward!" boomed a loudspeaker.

"Better do it," Abna murmured. "And I don't say I like things one little bit. Our host may have had an about face, but if you ask me he's still mighty dangerous."

"How does it happen that he's a small man?" Viona questioned.

"For that," the little man said, as the quartet approached the desk, "there is a simple explanation. In normal physique I am undersized and tiny—but large physique conveys an atmosphere of power, and authority. Those, of necessity, I must have. So it is a simple matter to project an image of an extremely tall, arresting-looking man."

"In other words, an inferiority complex of the nth degree?" Abna asked pointedly, then the next moment he was groveling on the mosaic stone floor, felled by a terrific mental blow.

"I do not like such remarks," the intellectual horror remarked, all trace of geniality gone from his face. "They approach close to saying that I am a madman, which obviously I am not. No madman could have such intellectual power."

The Amazon reflected swiftly, so swiftly her thoughts had not time to be read. Suppose this being really *were* mad, that he was some outcast of a race of superior thinkers working out his own egotistical destiny in isolation? If that were so, he might prove a dangerous foe indeed.

"So!" he commented, as Abna struggled up from the floor again. "You have conquered Time to investigate. You want to know what brought darkness to this region, and what created the eyeless race? I will tell you—I, and I alone, created the race!"

"For what reason?" the Amazon asked.

"For no other reason than to conquer the Universe— the vast and incomprehensible Universe! To make them the overlords of all other races and kinds.... From your point of view, the race has been created: from mine, it is yet to come. That is purely a Time paradox."

"But where's the sense in creating a race to conquer the Universe?" the Amazon demanded. "What do you get out of it?"

"I will tell you.... Satisfaction!" Thin hands clenched on the desk and the bright eyes glittered even more brightly. "A huge satisfaction, Golden Amazon. I, disgraced and an outcast of my people because of my progressive ways, will yet strike back. Not by myself, but by the children of my kind. The race yet to come."

The Amazon looked at Abna quickly and he caught her glance. He started speaking himself.

"You are speaking of a race which has yet to come: we are speaking from the viewpoint of having seen that race nearly a million years evolved—a cruel, eyeless, telepathic race.... But why in the name of the cosmos deprive them of light? The one most vital element necessary to progress? It doesn't make sense."

"That," the mental monster chuckled, "is where the subtlety comes in. I am going to give this race another sense to compensate for sight, which at once gives them immeasurable power. The power of being able to strike in the dark—absolutely to the heart. Nearly all races are sighted. In darkness, and without a sixth sense such as my race will have, they will be paralyzed. Imagine a world that normally has light. It is desired to conquer it....

"My race will have the power of creating darkness, the absolute cessation of all light by means of a spatial warp. Then, themselves not inconvenienced by darkness because they have a sense to compensate for it, they will strike without mercy. The race plunged into darkness will not be able to resist."

"And I assume," the Amazon asked, "that the gigantic object we call the Emerald plays a major part in all this?"

"Definitely...." The being became silent as if he were reflecting, then in his next words the true measure of his nature, and his madness, were revealed. "You wanted to examine the past, my friends, and see what it had to reveal. You shall do so. Without recourse to clumsy time machines or spaceships, I shall transport you to a time where the race is created—by synthetic means of my own devising—and you can view it firsthand. Be a part of it. And even die in it! In the early stages the race will be on this world, then later will move to the fourth planet from the sun. To transport you demands but a small effort of mental power, as you will see—"

And suddenly it was done, with such bewildering speed indeed that the four had hardly time to grasp it. Only slowly did the four begin to adjust their minds to the change....

The laboratory had completely vanished, and been replaced by towering jungle, a dense and alien labyrinth, seeming all the more weird and sinister by reason of the green sunlight shafting down here and there between the interlacings of foliage. The air was warm—even hot—and a restless wind stirred the exotic, waist-high bushes.

"Apparently our mental genius has succeeded in his object," Abna said at last, his voice grim. "And I don't suppose I need to drive home to any of you just what kind of a predicament we're in."

Viona and Mexone shook their heads slowly, but the Amazon made no response. She seemed to be lost in thought, regardless of the jungle around her.

"Anything the matter?" Abna asked curiously. "Apart from the obvious thing, that is."

"Can you integrate in seven dimensions, Abna?" the Amazon asked abruptly. "Using Tune and Space as your basic roots?"

"Seven dimensions? That's asking something. Makes the infinite calculus seem child's play by comparison. Why do you want to ask that, anyhow?"

"Just tell me: it may be vastly important."

"Er—yes. I can integrate in seven dimensions if need be."

"With Time and Space as the basic roots? Quickly! Before I forget."

"Yes." Abna stared. "What are you driving at, anyway?"

The Amazon did not answer. She pulled her foil-leaf notepad from her belt and quickly jotted down a formula with her stylus. Then with a sigh of relief she handed the hieroglyphics to Abna. He looked at them intently, then gave a puzzled glance.

"That," the Amazon explained. "Is all I can remember of the formula by which the mental monster transported us here. It is just the basic roots. I glimpsed them in his mind a second or two before we were transported, and I held them there. I'm a good mathematician, but integrating in seven dimensions has me beaten. Five is my limit—but since you say you can do it, it's all yours."

"What do you expect me to do from just these roots?"

"Work out how we get back. It must be possible by reversal. Our friend simply used a mathematical formula, which transported matter—otherwise us. If transportation can go one way, it must also go the other. It involves the reversal of all the figure bases, and then matter is bound to respond by very reason of having no mathematical basis to support it any longer."

She paused in her observation and looked about her. She could not be quite sure of it at first, but it seemed to her that the shady green sunlight was becoming dimmer, that the jungle was filling itself with unfamiliar shadows.

"Sunset?" Mexone asked, also becoming aware of the effect.

Abna peered intently through the skyward vegetation, then he shook his head.

"No, it's not sunset. Unless I completely miss my guess, we're viewing the beginning of the darkness—caused once again by that confounded Emerald."

They all of them stood quite still, trying to imagine what it was going to be like in this weird jungle without a vestige of light to guide them. And even as they conjectured, the green radiance of the sun gradually faded to black, whilst the shadows of the jungle became inky.

"Now what?" came the Amazon's voice out of the abyss. "The master-mind must have planned this, too! He selected a time very close to the darkness period, knowing that we would gradually come into it. It won't pass for tens of thousands of years, and we've no space-ship in which to devise a fresh neutralizer."

For a moment there was silence; then Abna spoke again. "Our only way to get back is to reverse the seven-dimensional formula, and I have no doubt that I could—but there's one thing against it."

"What's that?"

"You gave me what you remembered of the formula—the basic mathematical roots—on a sheet from your foil book. How am I supposed to read it in the dark?"

CHAPTER SIX
RETURN TO GREGOR'S WORLD

"That," the Amazon admitted, rubbing her tingling face and arms fiercely, "is certainly a problem as big as the formula itself. In a region where no light or warmth will operate we have to figure out how to get illumination...." She was silent for a long time, then finally she made the admission which she knew was inevitable. "I just don't know."

"Nor I," Abna muttered. "At this moment the gift of extrasensory perception would be a help."

"Wait a minute!" Viona exclaimed abruptly. "Maybe there's one way—a lot slower than we'd expected, but still possible. Give me the foil, dad."

There was a rustling and fidgeting in the darkness as Abna fumbled with his belt, then presently Viona felt the thin foil of metal thrust into her hand. Gently she fingered it and then gave an exclamation.

"Yes—we can do it! At least I can! The stylus you used, mother, has left indentations in the metal—as is only natural. I can just feel the raised ridges of the numbers and symbols you've executed. Here, feel for yourself."

The Amazon took the foil and gave a low murmur of satisfaction as her sensitive finger ends distinctly felt the indentations.

"I'll have to read it to you, Abna," she said. "You can memorize the figures as I give them?"

"Carry on," his voice said, and thereafter he listened in absolute silence as the Amazon reeled off the formula to him. It took her perhaps fifteen minutes, and when she had finished Abna repeated everything slowly while she 'read' the formula with her finger ends.

"Yes, that's it," she confirmed. "Now—can you do it?"

"Yes, but it's going to demand a pretty prodigious mental effort on my part to work things out. All of you stand close to me while I work it out, then you won't be beyond the area of my operations. Better still, hold my hands.... That's it. Now—not a sound out of any of you."

Obediently the others did as he instructed. Thereafter he was completely silent, using every ounce of his mental skill, even to the extent of forgetting he was a material living being. Had the others been able to see him during that intensive period they would have beheld an almost ethereal being, one so steeped in the profound complexities of mental power that he almost transcribed himself back into the original mathematical formula which had formed the basic pattern for his body.

Not being able to see him, the others could only sense what was happening. To the Amazon and Viona, who were each side of him and holding a hand each, the change in his physical constitution made itself felt by less solidity in the grip of his hand, then by a curious thrilling sensation like a powerful electric current. In those moments the trio had the feeling that they were being borne upwards into an abyss.

With the passing of the moments this sense of being mysteriously lifted upwards deepened until they were absolutely convinced that such was the case. With only the darkness, they had nothing to judge by—but the Amazon, at least, mentally following the processes of the mathematical formula she had given, was satisfied that Abna was accomplishing his object, and transcribing his immediate material surroundings back into the position they had occupied before the 'mastermind' had altered things.

Then suddenly they were in green sunlight, sunlight that was streaming through big windows.

"We did it," Abna murmured. "We're back in the mastermind's laboratory, the very point from which he dispatched us."

The others did not speak: they were too busy orientating themselves to the situation—to the realization that they had indeed been projected back again from the dangerous Time into which they had been hurled.... And, abruptly, the mastermind became conscious of their presence. He rose slowly to his small height, his beady eyes aflame.

The mastermind gave his slow; chilling laugh.

"That you have got back here represents a miracle—

but nevertheless I am prepared to accept it. But no further! You shall not have your *Ultra* back, and I think you know better than to try to cross your wills with mine."

"Certainly we do," Abna confessed with disarming frankness, "which is one reason why we have evolved another plan. It is quite simple— and yet effective!"

On the last words he suddenly leaped forward, so quickly that the mastermind had no time to anticipate what was coming—and when he did, it was too late. He was lying on his back on the laboratory floor, Abna's powerful hands clutching his neck—not tightly enough to strangle him, but certainly enough to produce violent pangs on the main nerve channels to the brain.

Swiftly the Amazon, Viona, and Mexone moved up, ready for action, but Anna shook his head at them.

"I fancy this is enough," he said grimly, pinning the dwarf down. "I don't know why we didn't think of it earlier.... Pain is an impossible enemy when you wish to concentrate. You cannot concentrate sufficiently to worry us, can you?"

The little man writhed and struggled desperately, hate and anguish both in his tiny eyes. Abna grinned faintly and increased the pressure. Automatically the pain increased and there came a series of gasping groans from the little man.

"I am not going to kill you because murder is against our general policy," Abna continued. "We'll kill only if we need to protect ourselves. This is just to prevent you getting enough mental force to wipe us out...."

Now, where is the *Ultra*?"

"Where—where you left it," the mastermind gasped. "I have not touched it. I swear that to you."

"It was in space when we were forcibly taken from it by your mind projection efforts. You mean that it is still there?"

"Yes.... Yes, where you left it."

Abna thought for a moment, then: "You value your life, my friend?"

Between spasms of violent pain the little man nodded.

"Very well then—you shall keep it if you do as I command. You will project my wife back to the *Ultra*, and let her bring the ship to us. For that purpose I will temporarily release you—but the instant you attempt anything contrary to orders, I'll kill you by sheer physical violence. The same thing applies if you attempt to send my wife anywhere but the *Ultra*. You understand?"

"I understand. I will do as you say."

"Prepared to risk it, Vi?" Abna asked, glancing at her—and she nodded.

"I'll do it, and be back here in record time."

"Right!" Abna relaxed his fingers even though he held them poised for instantly returning into position. "Proceed, mastermind! And remember what I've told you."

The little man, pale with fury and the pain he had been undergoing, raised himself on to one elbow and looked at the Amazon steadily. She returned his stare unflinchingly, her hand on her gun with the instinct of preparedness.

Moments passed—then very slowly the Amazon faded into thin air and was gone. Viona and Mexone looked about them anxiously, and Abna glanced at the mastermind.

"You have sent her to the *Ultra*?"

"I have—not because I want to, but because I have too much to do to die yet. And you, Abna of Jupiter, you have given me a great deal to think about. I shall spend much of my time when you have gone trying to fathom why mental might isn't always the master of physical violence."

Moments passed, and Abna still remained alert, never sure for a moment of the situation. Until at last there came a change as a huge, dark shape flashed past the giant windows, momentarily blotting out the sunlight.

"The *Ultra*?" Viona asked her father quickly, and he nodded.

"I believe so. We'll soon know."

The guess was right. After an interval of perhaps five minutes the Amazon appeared, her proton gun in her hand just in case.

"The *Ultra*'s outside," she said briefly. "I lowered it to the park in front of this building."

"You got aboard it all right?" Abna questioned.

"Yes. No trouble at all. One moment I was here, and the next I was emerging in the control room."

Abna began to move backwards, Viona and Mexone

doing likewise. When they reached the door where the Amazon was, Abna paused and looked toward the motionless mastermind. So far, as they had retreated, he had made no move. Perhaps the Amazon's gun was sufficient to dissuade him.

"How far away is the *Ultra*?" Abna murmured.

"About twenty yards. Down this main corridor outside here, and then we're in the open air. After that it's just one hop across a sort of quadrangle."

"Okay. Then let's make it as fast as we can. I don't trust this devil for a moment once we haven't got him under a gun."

"I'm ready when you are," the Amazon said.

"Let's go then."

With one concerted dive the four of them dashed into the corridor outside, and on that same instant the clawing hands of tremendous mental power sought to drag them down. As Abna had suspected all along, the mastermind had only been waiting until all threat of material superiority were removed before acting—and now indeed the quartet found themselves fighting his amazing powers with all the mental energy they had.

Faces distorted and gleaming with perspiration, they reached the outdoors, to behold the vast bulk of the *Ultra* near at hand. The power of the mental colossus was a screaming torment by this time, blasting and tearing the nerves, hanging thousand-ton weights on their feet. But somehow, hardly conscious of what they were doing, they kept on going. They gained the ship, and the ice cold of the metal work acted as a strange kind of stimulus.

"Inside," Abna said weakly, giving the Amazon a shove—and she went blundering helplessly into the control room, to collapse on the floor. Mexone and Viona followed her, and finally Abna himself.

By sheer main strength and a tremendous effort of will, he forced himself across to the control board and snapped the switch that closed the airlock. Then, senses reeling perilously, he grabbed the time-switch and pushed it off and on, thereby placing a month of time between the genius and themselves.

"As far as I can see, the only course now is to return to Gregor's world," the Amazon said. "We know precisely the conditions which are responsible for the greedy, ruthless ambitions of Arg and his people, and the only way to save them from themselves is to destroy that Emerald. Then, presumably, we shall stop the root of the trouble and there might be a little peace."

Abna nodded slowly, thinking; then presently he said: "Very soon we'll come back to the point where darkness descends, even as it did on the way here. We'll have to put up with it, of course."

Such indeed proved to be the case. At precisely the same point in the Time-track the darkness came, and there followed those wearying, vaguely terrifying hours as the cold slowly came with its steel grip. From their experience on the 'outward' journey, the quartet knew—at the speed they were traveling—that they would emerge from the cold and dark before things got too desperate, so they just hung on as best they could, leading that fantastic, groping existence to which they had accustomed themselves.

"Light's coming!" Viona cried finally.

"Yes, you're right," the Amazon breathed, her perfect figure dimly visible beside the great outlook window. "We're coming to the point in Time where our neutralizer banished the darkness—which means we haven't far to go. Better slow down, Abna."

He crossed to the control panel in a gray twilight, and five minutes later complete light had been restored, together with a comforting warmth as heat waves functioned once more. The Amazon continued to watch through the window, Viona and Mexone now at her side.

Everything looked exactly the same as it had at the outset of their experiences, with Gregor's bright, greenly lit world away to the left—near enough to produce an enormous segment of planet, toward which Abna turned the *Ultra*'s nose. Then, this done, he cut down the speed of the Time apparatus so that they were advancing at no more than two years to the minute. The amazing instrumentation then automatically performed the necessary calculations to ensure that they would land at approximately the correct time when they touched down on Gregor's world, conveying to Gregor the effect of having been away no more than a few minutes.

This definitely was the intention, but it did not work out in practice, for as the *Ultra* was swinging around for the final sweep that would carry it down to Gregor's world, darkness descended! It was so abrupt, so unexpected, that for the moment the four could not credit it. Then, realizing the danger, Abna turned from the utter blankness that was the window and felt his way to the control board.

"What has happened?" demanded the Amazon's voice. "According to our calculations, we ought to have landed approximately a few minutes after we departed from Gregor's world—and in full light! Where's the darkness come from?"

"Don't ask me," Abna replied. "Only thing I can think of is that Gregor's merry men have lost control of the spatial neutralizer we provided for them. That would bring darkness back right away. The fact remains that we're in it, and there it—"

He stopped suddenly as the *Ultra* shuddered violently, not from the impact of the landing—which automatic instruments had effected safely—but from the force of a tremendous shock wave. Quickly he switched off the Time mechanism.

"That's an explosion!" the Amazon exclaimed, staring uselessly into the blackness. "And a mighty powerful one, too. Nuclear, from the feel of it."

"Certainly fun and games are going on around here," Abna said grimly. "We'd better sit tight until it eases up a bit."

"Or go back in time to where there's a bit of light," Viona suggested.

"And what good would that do?" the Amazon demanded. "It's only evading the issue. We might just as well go out into space and never return here, leaving our job unfinished.… No, we've got to put up with this and see what we can make of it."

Another explosion shattered the ship's exterior as she finished speaking. Before the blast the *Ultra* moved several feet, pitching the four to the control room floor in the darkness. Unhurt, muttering to themselves, they struggled up again and waited for the next. Moments passed and nothing happened. A curious and unbelievable calm seemed to have descended.

"Looks like a lull," Abna said, after a moment or two. "Do you think it would be a good idea to open the airlock? There might be some of Gregor's people about, and they can come to us where we cannot see to go to them."

"Try it," the Amazon said—so after a moment or two there was the click of a switch as the great airlock swung wide. There came the sound of crackling— which was probably fire—and an acrid stench of explosives.

"Probably plenty of radioactive dust drifting in, and we can't do anything about it," the Amazon muttered. "Hear anything of people, Abna?"

"Can't hear anybody," he said presently. "For the time being, though, it does seem that the attack has stopped—"

"My friends, my friends! You have returned! Maybe there is some hope for us!"

"It's Gregor, isn't it?" Abna asked.

"Yes—of course it is Gregor. I had forgotten the

darkness! You cannot see me?"

"Not a single thing," the Amazon said bluntly. "What's been going on, Gregor? Where's the neutralizer we left with you?"

"It is badly damaged, friend Amazon—so damaged that we cannot repair it without your help. You had no sooner departed on your journey into Time before Arg launched an overwhelming attack on us. He has shattered most of our city, mainly because the blasting powers of the bombs have destroyed the upper surface and plunged below. There has been complete havoc, and tens of thousands of my people have been killed.... When you came back, he switched his attack to try to destroy you but fortunately he did not succeed."

"Not yet," the Amazon said. "If I know anything about Arg, he'll try again. We've got to do something quick."

"Your mission into Time?" Gregor's thoughts questioned. "Was it successful?"

"Very—but we've no time to talk of it now."

"What do we do, Abna?" the Amazon questioned.

"Get the neutralizer repaired," he answered promptly. "We can't possibly work in the darkness—"

"I will take you to it," Gregor said quickly. "Things are quiet at the moment, so we'll risk it. Give me your hand, Abna, and I will lead the way."

The journey on the whole was without incident, but they could tell by the number of enormous bomb craters they had to circuit how extensive the damage had been. From each of these, radioactive dust was presumably emanating, but at the moment there was nothing could be done about it. The Crusaders just had to go on, and hope their superhuman constitution would protect them in the short term.

"We are in what remains of one of the laboratories," came Gregor's thoughts. "This is where you left the spatial-neutralizer for us—and here it is. Let me guide you, friend Abna."

In another moment Abna found his fingertips touching the searing cold of metal. He recoiled instantly from that frigid bite and gave an apologetic smile into the darkness.

"I'm sorry Gregor—I cannot touch it. The cold is too severe. We'll need skin-tight gloves before tackling it."

"Then I'll have them manufactured immediately," came the response. "Stand here, my friends. I will return presently."

There came the sound of Gregor's footfalls receding into the darkness; then the Amazon spoke.

"Do you think it's going to be possible to repair this machine by touch alone, Abna? For myself I doubt it."

Abna said: "I can probably form an assessment of the damage by touch anyway. Once I have done that, can tell Gregor what to do in order to put things right."

It was nearly twenty minutes before Gregor returned, and then he thrust something cold and pliable into Abna's waiting hands.

"Gloves, friend Abna," he explained. "Synthetic calop, which in your language is the equivalent of rubber. Perhaps you will be able to feel the machine when wearing them."

"Thanks," Abna murmured, and pulled the gloves on. Then he experimented with the invisible metalwork. It still sent a thrill of cold even through the gloves, but it was possible to investigate without a gradually deadening numbness. So, little by little, he searched the exterior and interior of the machine, making mental notes of everything his hands 'saw.' At the end of half an hour his investigation was finished—and his hands were warm due to the insulation of the gloves.

"Damaged," he admitted. "But by no means beyond repair. In a few hours it can be put right, if you have about half a dozen experienced scientists who can work with you under my orders."

"That can be arranged immediately," Gregor promised. "I will see to it at once, friend Abna."

CHAPTER SEVEN
ASSAULT ON THE EMERALD

Before very long Gregor had summoned the required scientists to his side, and though the quartet could not see them, they could read from their varying thought waves that they were more than anxious and willing to help.

"Ready?" Abna inquired, when he sensed that Gregor was waiting.

"Yes, friend Abna. Tell us what to do and we will do it."

Abna wasted no more time. Entirely from his memory of the machine's original design, he gave instructions for replacement of vital parts, for rewiring of certain sections, and a hundred and one details which secretly left the Amazon amazed at the wealth of information he had stored up in his memory.

Then at last Abna's voice reached them. "We've got it, Vi! I have just checked everything and according to touch, it should be in order.... All right, Gregor— switch on the power!"

There was a brief interval, then came the familiar throbbing of power that told of the machine functioning normally. The quartet, their hands linked together, stood waiting and staring into the blackness.

"It ought to work," Abna said tensely, after a moment or two. "It's got to!"

He had just made the assertion when a grayness came over the face of things. In a matter of seconds it spread like a quick mist in which nothing was clear— then gradually a green glow began to penetrate from above, as through dispersing fog. A second or two longer and the green sun shafted through, bringing a glorious warmth at the same time. Simultaneously, the grayness went from ground level, and a vision of the wrecked laboratory became clear.

In the restored light the four gazed about them, inwardly shocked at the damage that had been wrought to a formerly well-equipped laboratory. The walls were standing, but the roof had been blasted away. Everywhere lay the ruins of instruments, of which very few had escaped destruction—and standing smiling beside the repaired spatial neutralizer were Gregor and his fellow scientists.

The Amazon's eyes lifted skywards as a vague black cloud began to form in the upper heights, catching the light of the green sun. Gregor turned his face skywards.

"A second attack! Take cover quickly!"

He motioned to the mountainous piles of rubble, of which there were all too many, and made a simultaneous dive toward the nearest one. In other directions Gregor's followers also departed hastily for whatever cover they could find.

The Amazon hesitated, staring skywards—and she still hesitated as Viona pulled at her arm.

"Quickly, mother! We've got to take shelter."

The Amazon did not move. She clenched her fists and then looked at Abna.

"The *Ultra*'s a long way off. Can't risk it," he said.

"You please yourself what you do, Abna, but I'm *going* to risk it. I never could hide from the enemy."

With that the Amazon darted away, staking everything on the fact that as yet Arg's fliers were still at a vast height. It would take a little time before they could come lower and be in a suitable position to open up an attack. On this the Amazon was risking everything, and although she was a naked target to the enemy far above, she kept on running with breathless speed, stumbling through the rubble of the upward slopes, dodging fallen girders, continually making her way upwards from the underworld without a single pause for breath.

She was nearing the rim of the underworld and Arg's circling fliers were breaking up into attack groups when Abna, Viona, and Mexone caught up. The Amazon flashed a glance at them as she raced onwards and Abna gave a broad grin.

"You don't think you're going to steal all the glory, do you?" he asked. "The Crusaders are a quartet, and that's the way it's going to continue."

The Amazon gave a grateful smile of thanks. With renewed energy she raced onwards, gained the rim of the underworld, then paused for a moment for breath.

She looked about her.

The *Ultra* was no more than half a mile distant, solitary and clearly visible, a perfect target for the screaming space machines that had now dropped to a dangerously low level overhead.

"Hurry up!" Abna cried, racing forward and catching the Amazon's arm. "They're getting us focused—"

By the very impetus of his speed he bundled the Amazon onwards, Viona, and Mexone pelting in the rear. They covered perhaps fifty yards toward the *Ultra* when Arg opened up his attack, not with bombs but with a series of varicolored rays. Everywhere they touched, rock and earth dissolved completely.

Nearer the *Ultra* came, and nearer. They were reeling within yards of it when the first bomb dropped. Fortunately, it was some distance behind them, but for a second they beheld their shadows clear cut on the ground before them as the incredible flash of light transiently drowned out the green sunlight. The blast lifted them from their feet and hurled them with savage violence against the *Ultra*'s outer plates.

Without speaking, Abna pushed the airlock button, und then he relaxed slightly, drawing the back of his hand over his streaming forehead.

"That explosion was nearly a mile behind us," he said at last. "A bit more on the target and—"

He got no further. Another bomb dropped, this time much nearer, and the *Ultra* rocked before the blast. The quartet jerked their eyes from the flash of unbearable light that momentarily flooded the windows; then they grasped whatever they could find to save themselves from falling.

"We'll move," Abna said grimly, switching on the power plant. "Much more of this and they'll hit the target—which is obviously the *Ultra*."

Moments later yet another bomb came. It was dangerously close—close enough to slew the mighty vessel around in a half circle and swamp it in livid flames of lavender and red; then it pulled free, jerked, and began to rise. For a while the incredible acceleration pressed them to the floor.

"That's better," Abna commented, putting in the automatic pilot and drawing a deep breath. "Now maybe we can think a bit more clearly as to what we are going to do next."

He helped the others to rise and they went over to the observation window. In that incredible leap they had covered millions of miles, leaving Gregor's world as a melon-sized planet in the gulf, while to the other side of the ship a solitary tennis-ball announced the presence of the outermost world—home of the Emerald.

"I suppose," Viona said, "we ought to go back and do battle with Arg? Wipe him out if possible."

The Amazon shook her head. "To do that would be to defeat our own ends. Our object is not to destroy the people of Dius—despite the violent attacks they have launched on Gregor's planet, and on ourselves. We want to rescue them from themselves and put an end to their constant desire for conquest."

"More plainly, destroy the Emerald?" Abna questioned.

"Exactly. And the sooner, the better. If Arg continues his attack on Gregor, even though he finds he has lost us, he may again hit the neutralizer, bringing back the darkness, which will make things immensely difficult for us. With the Emerald destroyed, the darkness will never return, since it is the main source and cause of it." The Amazon looked through the window, meditated for a moment, and then nodded. "Yes, that's our plan. Let's get going, Abna."

"Shall I head straight to the Emerald?" he asked, and the Amazon nodded.

"Might as well. The sooner it's destroyed, the better."

Abna kept his hands on the controls, viewing the scene through the window. It appeared exactly as it had on the first occasion that they had traveled here: the same desolate landscape, the twilight radiance of the distant green sun, and the endless hosts of stars spanning the void on every side.

None of the four said anything: they were too attentive to the exterior conditions. Then, finally, after perhaps twenty minutes—in which the *Ultra* flew slowly parallel with the surface at a height of about 2,000 feet—Viona gave an exclamation.

"There's the Emerald to the left! I can just see it."

The others saw it at the same moment—that 300-foot pyramid of bright green glass, or so it appeared to be. Abna headed towards it, finally passing right over it. Intently he studied it as it began to recede into the distance.

"How do we deal with it?" he asked, swinging around the ship's nose to make the return trip.

"Bomb it," the Amazon said, after thinking for a moment. "A medium-sized nuclear bomb ought to shatter it, and I don't think we need fear any unpleasant consequences from exploding it, either—in the way of dangerous vibrations and such, I mean. You keep the course, Abna, and I'll do the bombing."

He nodded and kept his attention on the controls, ready to make the vital spurt when the Amazon announced that she had released the bomb. She, for her part, stood in rigid attention at the bomb release mechanism, watching until the Emerald came directly in line with the prismatic sights. The first two runs were too much off center, so for the third time Abna had to make the run.

The Amazon watched the sights fixedly, then dead to the second she pressed the release button.

"Away!" she exclaimed sharply, and instantly the *Ultra* put on a sudden jerk of speed, hurtling away from the Emerald as the bomb went down.

The explosion, when it came a few moments later, was shattering. The twilight world was evanescently bathed in lurid brilliance, then to the accompaniment of rebounding shock-waves, rock and earth lifted skywards in a mighty column of destruction. Noise there was none, since there was no air to carry the sound-waves—but the resultant mushroom of smoke, climbing layer upon layer to the stars, showed quite clearly that the bomb had exploded as planned.

The *Ultra* lowered slightly and Abna reduced speed, crossing directly over the bombed area and through a haze of radioactive dust. He switched on the floodlights and the scene was a distinct jolt to the senses. In, fact, it was impossible! The Emerald was still there, part of the rock foundations alone having been shattered, but otherwise the thing itself was undisturbed.

The amazed Amazon turned from the window. "Bring the *Ultra* down, Abna."

This done, they left the ship for a closer look.

"The only conclusion to be reached is that this is not a normal form of matter, and therefore we—"

The Amazon glanced up. Something, for a moment, had cut across the green sunlight in a fleeting shadow. It was only momentary, but sufficient to distract her attention. Now she peered into the starlit bowl of sky in frank amazement.

Spaceships were there, dozens of them, cruising high above the plateau and gradually coming lower. A formation of them in crossing the sun had unexpectedly announced their arrival, since the noise of the rocket exhausts was, of course, cancelled due to the absence of air.

"Arg!" Abna exclaimed. "Somehow he's managed to follow us here—though how he knew this was our destination beats me. We'd better get back to the *Ultra* quickly. We've absolutely no protection against him."

He turned to go, the Amazon immediately behind him—but at the same moment the machines went into action, with their usual battery of varied rays. And they were so placed that they formed a solid screen of heat between the four and the *Ultra*. As one machine moved on, automatically taking its particular ray with it, another came to take its place.

Abna dragged to a stop and pulled out his proton gun. He gave the Amazon a grim glance.

"Looks as though we'll have to fight our way out," he said. "We can't possibly try and risk getting through those rays."

"Why do you imagine they haven't killed us already?" Viona asked, drawing her own gun. "They must be able to see us—and yet they don't blast us into kingdom come."

"There'll be a reason," the Amazon answered. "And I'll warrant it won't be a pleasant one, either."

No further words were exchanged as they concentrated their attention on watching the machines' slow descent. It was noteworthy that they came down in a circle—probably about fifty of them—thereby precluding any possibility of escape as far as the quartet were concerned. Finally they were settled and, their guns ready, the four stood watching as the airlock of one of the machines opened and a figure emerged. Due to the enveloping space suit he was wearing he was impossible to identify, but the quartet were fully prepared to believe it was Arg.

CHAPTER EIGHT
ARG'S CONVERSION

"It is interesting to meet you again, Golden Amazon," came his thoughts. "I detect that you didn't expect such a thing would happen."

"Correct," the Amazon retorted. "And we are rather at a loss to understand why you haven't killed us. Certainly it cannot be through lack of opportunity."

"True. You were nearly destroyed recently when you returned to Gregor's world, but that was without my knowledge. When I knew what was happening, I immediately gave orders for the attack to cease."

"And on the second occasion?" Abna asked grimly. "I assume that attempt to blow us to bits was again without your knowledge?"

"Not at all. The idea was to force you to surrender to us—to leave your spaceship. Our idea in dropping explosive all around you was to immobilize your machine. However, you escaped us with such tremendous speed we had no idea where you went."

"Yet you're here now?" the Amazon snapped.

"Certainly. The flash of an atomic bomb on this deserted world excited our curiosity, and we came immediately to investigate.... And now—" Arg's thoughts slowed down to sinister deliberation.

"I think we can pick up the thread where we left off. For that reason only have you been spared from death. I still wish to know how you control space so brilliantly, to the extent of restoring light and heat. You will recall you were on the point of revealing it when—for the moment—you outwitted us."

"We were never about to reveal anything," the Amazon snapped. "And we never shall be."

"That, friend Amazon, remains to be seen. Our powers of persuasion are by no means exhausted, and we mean to have that information. Once we have it, we can dispose of you. It is not our wish to destroy your *Ultra*: it contains so many valuable secrets embodying a science which is foreign to us, that we would be foolish to throw opportunity away when it is given to us."

The Amazon's eyes strayed to the *Ultra*, still cut off by the wall of machines. She said nothing.

The others looked at her as though waiting for a lead, then when they did not get it, they relaxed with hands still tight on their guns.

"I don't happen to know the power of the weapons you are carrying," Arg's thoughts continued. "Nor can I read the information from your minds. Rather than take chances, I order you to drop them."

The four remained motionless, whereupon, after a moment or two, Arg raised a bloated arm in a signal. The instant he did so the quartet felt power leave their limbs to such an extent they nearly fell flat on the rocky ground. In any event, their weapons dropped from nerveless hands, and they found they could not budge themselves an inch forward or backward.

"I do not propose to wait any longer for the information I seek," Arg's thoughts resumed, after a pause. "This young one amongst you—Viona, I think you call her—knows as much as you do, I imagine. Even if she doesn't, it is possible the sight of her sufferings will break down the obstinacy of you, Golden Amazon, and you, Abna. At least we can see."

The Amazon tried to move, but failed. Abna also attempted to put himself at Viona's side, but he was completely immobilized, Something was obviously being generated from one of the ships—no doubt Arg's own—which produced a form of paralysis.

"To continue," Arg proceeded, pulling a sharp knife from his space suit belt. "My intention is to puncture a tiny hole in your daughter's space suit. The air pressure within it will slowly lower, bringing to her the effect of slow suffocation. Whether she dies or not is up to you, or her. And surely I do not need to add that the escape of air from her suit will produce other unpleasantness? Such as the bursting of the body from inward pressures upon the external zero...." The 'tone' of his thoughts changed. "What is it to be, Golden Amazon? Abna?"

The Amazon and Abna exchanged troubled glances, but they did not attempt any move, or speech. Whereupon Arg turned to the completely helpless Viona and prodded at the hard rubber and metal composition of her space suit. As a matter of fact, he prodded too hard and, being unable to move or help herself, Viona toppled backwards and overbalanced. Since she was slightly on a downslope she rolled a few feet away, bouncing in her inflated suit—and that brought a surprising revelation to her. She could move normally! All her limbs and muscles were functioning again.

For a moment she was tempted to get up, then she thought better of it. Obviously she had fallen beyond the influence of whatever it was being radiated, and as things were now she was the only hope of the four. The rest of them were looking down at her from their slightly higher positions, still unable to budge even a finger.

Then Arg came striding down the slope. It was curious that he, too, was not affected by the radiation; probably there was some form of insulation in his space suit. He paused, finally, only a foot away from the fallen Viona, and she could see the sneering smile on his eyeless face as once again he raised his knife to drive it into her space suit.

Tensed for action, she waited until he stooped toward her; then suddenly her arm flashed up, gripped his inflated forearm, and down she pulled with all her strength. With a steel grip on his arm, and the girl's feet shoving hard into his middle, Arg could do nothing else but go flying right over her in a wild somersault. He crashed into the rockery, knife flying out of his hand; he had no chance to get up again, for Viona whirled forward to the attack, a clumsy, bouncing figure. In a matter of moments Arg found himself pinned down with her gloved hands digging with relentless force into his throat.

"Drop and roll!" she yelled to the others, through her audiophone. "Let yourself fall! You'll get out of the influence that way."

They did not question things: they acted. The moment they dropped to the rockery, they automatically bounced down the slope, then began to pick themselves up again. The Amazon was first on her feet, and she came over to where Arg lay helplessly.

"What do I do?" Viona demanded, glancing up. "Choke the life out of him?"

The Amazon shook her head inside her helmet. "No, Viona, that isn't our way of doing things."

Somewhat reluctantly Viona obeyed. The Amazon stood in the girl's former position, but she did not make any attempt to lay her gloved hands on Arg—until he got to his feet. Then abruptly she leaped nimbly behind him and locked one hand securely in the belt around his space suit.

"We're going back to the *Ultra* to discuss things, Arg," she said curtly, "and you're coming with us so that we can be assured no harm will be done us. Your followers will not dare to attack while you are with us. Go ahead of me, and give orders for their fire to be withheld."

Arg marched forward as she nudged him, pausing again as the Amazon jerked him to a standstill while she picked up her proton gun from the rockery. The others did likewise, and then progress resumed.

Passing between two of the spaceships, they came finally to the *Ultra*. The Amazon led Arg into the control room, then she gave a nod to Abna, and the airlock closed. Left to himself, Arg stood and waited; then as she jerked off her space suit, the Amazon said:

"Get your suit off, Arg. You don't need it in here."

He obeyed, then slowly settled himself as the Amazon nodded towards a seat. She, too, sat down, with Abna, Mexone, and Viona to either side of her.

"The time has come, Arg, to discuss vital matters," she said quietly. "You understand?"

His thoughts were affirmative even though his austere face was grim.

"The issue between us is that you think the Universe should be dark so you can continue with your conquests without undue opposition. We believe, on the other hand, that there should be light, and that you should live in friendship with your neighbors and abandon your ideas of conquest. In fact, we intend to see that you do.... Your desire for conquest is begotten of only one thing—the huge radioactive emerald on this planet."

The Amazon read a variety of thoughts in Arg's mind, but none of them was clear. Hostility, the desire for understanding, fear—all the emotions were there.

"You do not conquer because it is your innermost wish," the Amazon stated deliberately. "You conquer because your emotions are raised to that point by the Emerald's radiations! At least do me the honor of admitting it, as one scientist to another."

"Very well," came the clear-cut thought. "I admit it. It is an artificially produced stimulus, and there is no way to break it. How it came about we don't know."

"We do," the Amazon responded. "We have traveled backwards in Time to find out. You and your race, Arg, are nothing more than the servants of a vengeful, super-brilliant scientist who created you solely that you could exact vengeance on the rest of the Universe. The desire to kill, plunder, and conquer is not your ambition, but his. Through the Emerald and its satanic powers you are compelled to obey. It is not the real Arg who is doing it."

"Your words do not make sense, Golden Amazon. What of the other race on Gregor's planet? They are part of us and we are part of them. Yet they do not conquer. They are fools, who live in peace."

"They live in peace, Arg, but they are not fools. They are less affected by the Emerald than yourselves. However, to get to the point: we are determined to make you and your race live as normal people, in a lighted, warm universe. We are going to turn your idea of universal conquest into an empty dream—purely for the sake of the Universe and yourselves. We are going to destroy the Emerald."

The thoughts of Arg crystallized abruptly into an unmistakable pattern of hate.

"You shall not destroy what you call the Emerald. It is our god, and we will not allow it."

"So that is the situation?" the Amazon said slowly.

"Although you know this Emerald is prompting you to do things which are really against your nature, you are nevertheless prepared to worship it as a deity?"

"You are clever scientists. That I admit, but even you cannot carry out your project to destroy our god. Nothing can destroy anything that is conceived out of a thought formula. How else do you account for the Emerald's indestructibility?"

"We have tackled crystallized thought before in our adventures," Abna mused. "I admit it was not of the same order as this, but crystallized thought just the same."

"Which obviously cannot be destroyed," Arg's thoughts proclaimed, with an air of absolute finality.

"That is your hope, my friend," Abna retorted. "You want to believe that we are beaten, so that your god cannot be destroyed—but such is not the case. A creation of thought *can* be destroyed, by yet another formation of thought, and that is the line we intend to take."

Arg's thoughts ceased, which seemed rather surprising. He seemed to be listening for something, his head cocked. In a second or two the four began to realize what was attracting him....

A thin, high note was coming from somewhere outside the ship, increasing in pitch with every second that passed.

"That's an ultrasonic beam unless I miss my guess," the Amazon said abruptly. "And of considerable danger to the *Ultra* and us—"

"Exactly so," Arg interrupted. "When I gave my signal a little while ago, you had no idea what my thoughts were at the time—thoughts which were received by my immediates-in-command. I said that if I did not reappear within a short time—I think five of your minutes was the exact time—then the *Ultra* must be destroyed—and me within it. You as well! That process is now under way."

The Amazon swung abruptly and switched on the power plant, Abna's eyes followed her in surprise. She waited a second or two until the instruments registered the maximum load on the power plant, then she went to the switch-panel and made further adjustments. The *Ultra* seemed to jolt very slightly, and outside the ultrasonic humming ceased.

"What have you done?" came Arg's venomous thoughts.

"Put a month of time between ourselves and your men, my friend. As things are now, they haven't even arrived on this planet. You overlooked the fact we have a time-machine aboard this ship."

"Nice work!" Abna grinned, "I'd forgotten all about that." He strode to the window and looked out on to the bare plateau. "You're right, too! Not a ship in sight. That's something you didn't reckon with, Arg!"

Arg relaxed slowly, controlling himself. For a moment or two his thoughts were unintelligible, but his eyeless countenance showed the bitter chagrin he was experiencing.

"I am not fool enough not to know when I have met

my masters," his thoughts said finally, with a tinge of bitterness. "I have to accept the fact that you are cleverer than I. I have tried by all scientific means to outwit you, and every time you have beaten me. A leap back into Time itself is something which I cannot cope with...." His thoughts changed to quiet resignation. "I am ready, if you wish to dispose of me. I cannot fight you any longer."

"We have no wish to destroy you," the Amazon replied. "You are far too clever a man to be disposed of, even if we wished it. But most certainly we are going to destroy your god, and give you and your race the chance to behave as your normal will dictates, We want you to help us, if you will. If you do not, it will only make the struggle harder, because we're going to need every assenting mind we can get."

"Every assenting mind?" Arg's thoughts asked. "What do you intend doing?"

"Going back into Time still further, back to contact the genius who created this god of yours, and getting from him the formula that brought it into being. When we have that, we can work out the solution as to how to destroy it. This creature we are going to contact is the master of thought, and a deadly enemy. With thought alone we can deal with him. Give us your word to behave quietly and normally while we make the journey. You will not attempt anything likely to upset our plans or calculations?"

"I give you my word."

The Amazon nodded, inwardly satisfied. Turning to

the switchboard, she adjusted the controls of the time-apparatus and then applied the power. In silence Arg watched the misty kaleidoscope of scenes drifting by outside the window, until presently they increased to a no longer intelligible blur.

"We have a long journey ahead of us," Abna remarked presently. "Close on a million years—which means many hours. We had better have a meal."

So it began—the usual waiting period. No new experience for the quartet, but definitely something different for Arg. Evidently, he seemed to realize he was the odd man out, for he refrained from thought transmissions and kept mainly to himself.

Against the huge observation window sat Arg, a silent figure, his whole attention on the view outside—which, when it became steady, revealed a long grass plateau, distant mountains, and a glowing green sun. Abruptly the time-mechanism clicked and the journey across a million years was over.

"Have we arrived?" Arg's thoughts inquired presently.

"Definitely," the Amazon assured him. "Since our vessel has not moved in space, it is occupying a position normal to it for a million years back in Time. Formerly we were on rockery; now we are on a grassy slope. We see the outermost planet as it was a million years ago." She glanced at the display. "Purposely, we have arrived a little later than on the former trip we made. We ought to be at the approximate time of the creation of your race."

"But there is nobody here. Nobody in sight. No cities, no sign of habitation," Arg transmitted.

"If the genius is still here, he will find us," the Amazon said confidently. "Then you will realize something of his power. If by mischance we have come to a point where he has departed, then we must find our way further back until we contact him.... Let us wait for a while and see what happens."

It was plain from his thoughts that Arg was having difficulty in seeing how there might be life on the planet, but he passed no comment. He waited, as did the quartet, for something to happen.

Minutes passed, and nothing did.

"Maybe we're wrong," Abna said at last. "On the previous occasion we had the manifestation of a city, and then the thought projection. This time there is neither—yet I imagine that wherever we landed on this planet the genius would detect us, granting he was present."

"And he's even had dealings with us before," Viona put in. "So at least we're not strangers to him. Had we landed in an earlier Time, I suppose we would be...."

"Earlier or later," a voice interrupted. "It makes no difference. I remember you well, my friends, and not with any great pleasure, either.... But I do not remember the fifth among you. Who is he?"

"One of the race you created, come back to question you," the Amazon replied curtly.

Arg had turned now, and his eyeless face was registering complete amazement at the size of the apparition. As the Amazon turned to him for confirmation of her words, Arg's thoughts came forth. They were confused, and it was plain he was having a struggle to keep a grip on himself.

"The Golden Amazon tells me," his thoughts ran, "that you are the creator of the green god whom we obey. Is that correct?"

"It is correct," the stony voice replied. "And it is only owing to the childish ingenuity of these four travelers that you have been enabled to come back and thus question your creator." There was a grim pause for a moment, and then the entity continued: "I made every endeavor to crush you, my friends, last time you were here—but you eluded me. I am surprised that you have come back, for this time I shall not let you defeat me. You did it last time by physical violence. But this time I shall be prepared."

Abruptly, as on the earlier occasion, there came the clamping force of that awful mind. Arg visibly staggered before it as he got up from the position by the window. He took three steps and then dropped flat on his face. The quartet noticed his collapse, but they had far too much to grapple with to pay any heed to him. They concentrated as never before, throwing every mental effort they possessed into an effort to upset the mind's influence. By degrees they could feel themselves weakening—and as this happened, the Amazon made a last tremendous effort. Turning, she reeled toward the switch panel and groped for the Time control.

Overpowering forces sought to prevent her pulling

the time switch, which was certainly her intention—
yet inch by inch her yellow hand reached towards it.
Her face was a frozen mask of strain, perspiration
streaming down it from the mental effort she was
making. Abna, Viona, and Mexone turned to help her,
but there they remained, chained to the spot.

Suddenly the switch clicked, and instantly the alien
influence of that mind vanished, as did the apparition.
The Amazon straightened, pulled the switch again,
and then gave a grim smile.

"A year between us and the genius," she commented.
"That gives us time to think."

"About what?" Abna asked bluntly. "I begin to
think there's nothing we can do about the situation,
Vi. We thought Arg might be a help to us in offsetting
the genius, but he was the first to collapse. As for us,
we just can't risk it. He'll beat us in the end with the
terrific mental power he has at his disposal."

"He won't if our counter-thoughts are amplified,"
the Amazon responded. "That was one reason why I
moved us into Time to gain a brief respite. For a matter
of fact, the idea comes from the mind of the genius
himself. I saw it there, even as he was trying to crush
us."

Abna, Viona, and Mexone all looked mystified, so
the Amazon went on to explain.

"There was a dominant thought in the mind of the
genius even as he tried to overpower us. It was—'Why
don't these fools think of amplifying their thoughts
and protect themselves? But then, what can one expect

of the lower orders of intelligence?' That was the thought—or something like it. Now I'm wondering why we never thought of it ourselves."

"A thought-amplifier!" Abna exclaimed "Why, of course! In that way we can increase the power of our thoughts 100 or 1,000 times as required."

"Exactly." The Amazon turned and helped Arg to his feet as he showed signs of recovery. When he had straightened up, his thoughts came forth.

"I shall raise no objection," Arg's thoughts came. "I have seen for myself, and I know now that all you have been telling me is true. My only wish now is to have my own will in control, and not that of a being whose only ambition is to destroy."

"Good!" The Amazon gave a relieved smile and then held out her hand. "From now on, then, you with us?"

"Entirely," came the thought, and the handclasp was firm and sincere.

CHAPTER NINE
THE ULTIMATE WEAPON

Though the Amazon had only glimpsed from the genius' mind that an amplifier was needed—and no details whatever as to how to construct such an instrument—her imagination and scientific skill were fired enough to supply the necessary technical requirements. With the help of Abna—and in a less spectacular way that of Viona and Mexone also—she set to work to work out the details; and so there began one of those long, sleepless, scientific arguments that gradually resulted in the first designs of a workable mechanism.

The scientific wrangling continued on and on as various modifications were suggested, but in the space of another three hours, everything was hammered out to satisfaction—then after a sleep during which Mexone and Viona took over the watch, Abna and the Amazon rose to commence the actual construction of the instrument their amazing brains had conceived.

Within six hours the job was done, the complicated result being contained in a black container no larger than a cigar box. On one side of it was a projection, a lensed snout from which the amplified thought waves would emanate; while on the top of the apparatus was a slowly revolving, perfectly balanced, wafer-thin plate of copper—the actual magnetic brain-pan which would pick up the thoughts as they were transmitted from any area within six feet. The thing was a masterpiece of ingenuity, and judging from its enormous hypnotic power when on test against Abna, it was also an unqualified success.

"Good!" the Amazon exclaimed, when the tests were complete. "I think we'll give the genius a run for his money this time. The sooner we find out, the better. Everybody ready?"

The others, including Arg, nodded promptly.

So, without wasting any further time, the Amazon moved to the switchboard, started up the power, and set the *Ultra* cruising swiftly back toward the cloud-wrapped outermost world.

"Since it is of no particular concern which of us wears this amplifier," Abna said, watching the distant planet very slowly increasing in size, "I suggest that I take it. If the genius is able to strike, he will obviously choose the person carrying the amplifier, and as the leader of this quartet—"

"We're joint leaders," the Amazon interrupted him. "I created the original idea of the Cosmic Crusaders. I'll take the responsibility myself."

"But, Vi—"

"Perhaps a neutral would be best?" came the thoughts of Arg. "Why not let me take it? I would like some kind of dangerous responsibility, if only to make amends for the way I've doubted you in the past. If there should be any danger, then let me face it."

As neither the Amazon nor Abna answered, he moved across to the box and strapped it comfortably about his neck; then he added:

"From your earlier discussions, I assume that so long as I remain within six feet of you, the instrument will pick up your thought waves—and mine—without difficulty?"

"No doubt of it," Abna agreed. "We had hardly expected that you would take such a step to help us."

"Why not? Now I have seen the deception for myself, my only desire is to be rid of this green god which has, since my birth, dictated all my motives."

There was obviously nothing more to be said; Arg was completely converted, but no matter how great his personal willingness to renounce all ideas of conquest, he did not stand a chance as long as the Emerald existed. And this was the thought that dominated the minds of the quartet as they watched the outermost world sweep ever nearer.

They all waited tensely for something to happen as the Amazon brought the *Ultra*'s huge mass down gently on a sloping valley side. Then, as the power plant cut off, they began their survey.

"I don't remember seeing this valley before—or for that matter any of this landscape," Abna commented, after a moment. "Not that it signifies. I imagine that the topography of this world changes as rapidly as the genius alters his thoughts. In any case—"

He stopped dead, aware of changes outside. The others were at his side, including Arg, his eyeless face pressed against the big observation window. Changes there certainly were, merging rapidly into concrete form. There was first a misty suggestion of walls, which rapidly took shape into the real thing. Walls of unbroken metal, towering far above the *Ultra* in height—and suddenly there was a roof, which shut out the sunlight. Instead, enormous arcs of tremendous power blazed from various points. Then came instruments, bank on bank of them, stretching into the light-drenched distance, at which point the vision became steady. Out of nowhere, a vast hangar equipped with instruments had been created, and so rapidly that the five in the *Ultra* had hardly had a chance to keep pace with developments.

"Wonder what the idea is?" Abna muttered, and not a second after he had asked the question there came a familiar booming voice—but on this occasion there was no projection accompanying it.

"The idea is simple, my friends. I intend to destroy you, your ship, and everything connected with you. Your vessel at the moment is in the foci of four instruments, each of them able to project a disintegrating beam that will demolish you. I allowed you to approach and settle unmolested, and then I created this impregnable laboratory around you. You cannot escape, and I have you pinpointed. As I said earlier, you are fools—utter fools. Do you think for one moment that I don't know about your thought amplifier? Your minds are nakedly exposed to me. Your destruction shall commence at this moment!"

The voice ceased. For an instant there was a dead silence in the control room; then the Amazon dived to the switch panel and slapped over the airlock control. The ponderous door began to open.

"What's the idea?" Viona asked in surprise.

"We're going outside, getting clear of the *Ultra* in case it should be destroyed. We've run into a trap, but we're not done yet. Quickly, outside!"

The others did not hesitate another moment. One after the other they followed the Amazon through the airlock into the drenching floodlight of the metal-bound hangar. And it seemed that the Amazon's prescience was justified, for within a few seconds the *Ultra*'s enormous mass began to shudder as invisible vibratory waves were trained upon it, Crouched, feeling the waves beating about them, the five watched the incredible phenomenon of the *Ultra* shivering into nothing. It became misty, transparent, and then was no more. There was nothing left but the vast hangar and its blazing light. Shielding her eyes, the Amazon looked under her hand into the brilliant distances. Then abruptly she gripped Abna's arm as he peered too, beside her.

"There he is!" she whispered. "Across there beside that tall machine, and evidently he hasn't seen us. Nor is his mind searching for us, probably because he believes we faded out with the *Ultra*. That must be his control panel."

The others looked, and because of the effulgence, it took them a while to pick out the tiny figure that was undoubtedly that of the genius. When at last he was sighted, Arg's thoughts took on a tinge of incredulity.

"Is that little creature the genius? Surely you are mistaken?"

"By no means," the Amazon answered. "His projection of a big, regal man is purely a build-up. Actually, he's small.... And we have got to tackle him before he becomes aware of us. He'll do so the moment he brings his mind to the task. Switch on that amplifier, Arg."

Arg obeyed, and at that the Amazon jerked her head. Then she moved swiftly, with the ease of a tigress, across the intervening space. When she was twelve feet away the mastermind turned suddenly, aware of her. She did not hesitate. She sprang with all the force of her leg muscles, her hands extended for action. The little man had not the chance to prepare himself, either mentally or physically. He went down before her rush, and in another moment she was astride his chest, one fist raised to deal a smashing blow if necessary.

Abna, Viona, Mexone, and Arg came up quickly, then paused as they saw the situation. For a moment or two the little man glared, then suddenly his mental resistance came into action. In spite of herself, the Amazon felt her mind clouding under a tremendous mental pressure.

"This time," she said, gazing steadily back into the blazing eyes, "it is not going to be so easy—as you will see."

With that she gave a brief signal to the others; then she hurled every ounce of her concentration forth in an effort to beat the mental waves threatening to overpower her. With the mind force of the four others added, and the amplifier in operation, the effect was immediate. The genius relaxed his compulsion and visibly writhed as though undergoing physical torture.

"Satisfied?" the Amazon asked, relaxing a trifle. "You've only yourself to thank for this! Back of your mind just recently was the thought of an amplifier. Now we're using it, with good results. We intend to destroy the Emerald with which the races of the future—the races you have yet to create—are controlled. Here is a representative of that race, who wants to live his own life, not the life you have set out for him."

"The green stone cannot be destroyed," the genius replied stubbornly.

"Not by material means," the Amazon agreed. "We have already tried that, and failed. But mental powers can destroy it because it is composed of thought itself, crystallized. Whether you have yet made the stone doesn't signify. We cannot alter what Time has written. But we can, and will, destroy it in the future, at a period when this world is deserted and dead. From you we want its formula, the formula of its composition."

The little man remained motionless, his enormous forehead furrowed and his eyes expressing the unholy fury that ruled him. Then as the Amazon concentrated—only slightly—into the amplifier about Arg's neck a look of pain came to the puckered features.

"Very well," he muttered. "I will give you the formula, though I doubt if minds in your low state of development will be able to understand it.... Here it is."

He started speaking and the Amazon flicked the button of the minute tape-recorder on her belt. Every word was instantly recorded, but even she was amazed at the complex profundity of the mathematics involved. For quite seven minutes the genius was talking, giving every detail, every fraction, every equation. Then he silenced and aimed his sharp eyes at the Amazon.

"Satisfied?" he asked coldly.

"By no means," the Amazon answered bitterly. "Now I have got the formula, I demand the means to put it into effect. You are the master of material things, therefore you will recreate the *Ultra* exactly as it was before your beams destroyed it."

The little man's face was stubbornly determined as he shook his immense head. At that the Amazon nodded to the others, and then concentrated all her thoughts into the amplifier. They were thoughts of invincible power, of conquering science, of everything guaranteed to make the mastermind aware of his immense inferiority.

Amplified as they were in power, and coming from five people at once, the little man stood no chance. He reeled under the impact and dropped to the floor, beating it in frenzied anguish with his small fists as lethal barb after lethal barb crashed into his anguished brain. Within seconds he knew that sanity was tottering.

"I'll do...as you order," he whispered, great drops of sweat coursing down his haggard face.

The Amazon switched off the amplifier, and then folded her arms. In majestic coldness she waited.

Slowly the genius recovered himself and struggled up from the floor. Then gradually he got himself sufficiently in hand to concentrate, and strange indeed was the result thereof. Under his uncanny mastery of material forces the outline of the well-remembered *Ultra* began to appear within the enormous hangar, and within five minutes the creation was complete. Very slowly the genius relaxed and passed a hand over his wide forehead.

"Congratulations," the Amazon said, in genuine admiration. "Now we shall keep our word and leave you in peace. This has been an unusual experience for you, mastermind. Five people, far less than you in intellect, have nevertheless beaten you."

The genius did not reply, but still stood with his hand to his forehead, apparently trying to recover from his creative effort. The Amazon glanced at the others and then hurried quickly to the *Ultra*. The others bundled after her through the airlock.

Abna turned to the Time-control. He switched it over and after a second or two of blurry unreality the mighty walls and roof outside faded and were replaced by the fast-moving interweave of advancing moments, hours, and presently days as the speed increased.

"Right!" the Amazon said, turning from the incomprehensible view. "Let's get to work. Easiest way will be to feed the whole formula to the *Ultra*'s master computer brain and let it sort things out."

It was about this time that the darkness shut down again. The mad view outside dissolved into blackness and the lights of the computer brain faded from sight. From then on the five had to possess their souls in patience while, out of the abyss, the computer hummed rhythmically.

Long before the blackness lifted, the brain had ceased its calculations and given a final beep, which announced that it had arrived at a solution.

Onwards and onwards, never moving in space, but hurtling through Time now at the maximum velocity of fifty years to the minute. Down went the temperature. There were periods of sleep, fumbling meals, hours of chafing impatience.... Then at last the oblivion began to lift, and hazy green sunlight came through the dispersing blackness. Further forward in Time the *Ultra* went, until finally its preset controls operated, and the blurry chaos outside resolved abruptly into a steady picture. Immediately the five looked through the observation window.

They were motionless on an immense shelf of rock overlooking the gaunt, friendless reaches of the deserted outermost planet. The unfamiliar stars glinted down in icy desolation.

The Amazon turned to the computer and removed from it the printout that contained the answer to the problem. She studied it, her brows knitted, with Abna gazing over her shoulder.

"It can't be right!" she exclaimed at last. "It just can't be. All that enormous mass of mathematics to be dissolved by zero raised to the infinite power?"

Abna looked at the answer. It said simply: 'Zero raised to the power of infinity equals dissolution.'

"Something's wrong with the machine," Viona decided; "Probably we gave it so many equations it's got mathematical indigestion."

"May I look?" came Arg's thought waves, and the Amazon handed him the sheet.

"I do not pretend that my mathematics equal yours," he said, finally, his thoughts clear and distinct. "But it does seem to me that in any form of computation the result is cancelled out by the application of the minus symbol. Nothing can exist when faced with an overwhelming negative, and even less can a creation of thought...such as the Emerald. Yes, I think it is correct."

"All we can do is try," the Amazon shrugged, picking up the amplifier, which Arg had long since discarded. "We can concentrate a zero impulse through this amplifier, all five of us, and step it up to maximum power. We'll see what happens.... Let's be on our way, Abna. And you'd better cut off our repulsive shield."

Abna brought the *Ultra* gently down within fifty yards of the Emerald. Turning again to the window, he surveyed the enormous 300-foot mass of what looked like green glass.

"Are we ready?" he asked, glancing at the Amazon.

She placed the amplifier in a convenient position on the window seat and then said:

"Ready, yes—but we'd better take certain precautions. We don't know the power of what we're going to release, or what will take place. In case we need to make a quick departure I should leave the power on, Abna. Then we can still save ourselves."

He obeyed, surveyed the instruments, and then signaled to Viona and Mexone. In response they came close beside him, and the Amazon and Arg also joined the group.

"We know what we have to do," he said quietly, surveying the huge mass through the window. "Concentrate on the zero quantity and leave the handling of the amplifier to me. Concentrate when I give you the word."

The others nodded and watched Abna switch on the amplifier. Then he moved the power-pointer to the maximum position and gave a nod, at the same time making sure that the lensed end of the amplifier pointed in the direction of the Emerald. Simultaneously all five concentrated with all their power—

The result was staggering, and incredibly swift. First the Emerald itself dissolved like a thing of mist before the shaft of negative thought hurled at it. It was so rapid the five had hardly time to grasp it before it happened. Nothing could stand under the million-fold zero concentration for the simple reason that it denied the existence of matter itself!

With the disappearance of the Emerald, the rocks

themselves began to disappear. A vast gorge opened up, deepening with every second. It became deeper and forced a colossal cleavage in the plateau, exactly covering the area bounded by the amplified thought waves.

Where the destruction would have ended there was no telling, but abruptly realizing the frightful power they had unleashed, the Amazon reached out and switched off the amplifier. Then she stood looking at the tremendous chasm that had been produced. It went down to incomputable depth, and stretched in a clean-cut line to the star-powdered horizon.

"Enough of that!" she whispered, "A few seconds longer and the whole planet would have been cut in half! We've destroyed the Emerald, and that was our main purpose."

"And we have found a weapon surpassing anything we ever possessed before," Abna breathed.

"A weapon of pure thought, based on the zero cancellation. There is nothing material in the universe that can stand against us. All our other weapons, even the proton gun, are a child's toys by comparison."

* * * * * * *

A week later, after the celebrating on Gregor's world was over—and complete union between him and Arg had been established—the *Ultra* took off and rapidly climbed to the heights.

Once in space, they examined the nearby star clusters, choosing a section of the heavens that looked worth investigating. Then the Crusaders relaxed into sleep as the *Ultra* built up speed and then slipped into hyperspace, enabling them to hurdle the interstellar gulf at a speed faster than light, before dropping back into normal space. The Crusaders were automatically awakened. The Amazon was the first to the observation area.

"A fresh area for investigation," she murmured, moving to the telescope. "Let's see if there's anything interesting.…"

Her violet eyes searched the depthless mysteries of the Milky Way, the mighty First Galaxy, with its spawning myriads of worlds—then at last, quite by chance, she singled out one planet in particular. It was pale green in color and hovered in isolation many millions of miles distant.

"That looks attractive, and green seems to be our color at the moment," she laughed. "See if it suits us, Viona."

Viona hurried over to the telescope as the Amazon moved aside. She refocused the instrument as she studied the planet intently. At length she gave a long whistle of incredulity. Instantly the Amazon, Abna and Mexone turned from the window.

"What is it?" Abna asked in surprise.

"I think I'm seeing things," Viona answered uncertainly, getting up from the lens. "Take a look for yourselves."

One by one the others did so, and then they looked at each other in wonder.

"It doesn't make sense!" the Amazon declared. "That planet is Earth! The features are identical, even to the outlines of the continent and cities. Earth, just as we left it many years ago.... She went to the window and surveyed the stars. "And yet we are countless light years, perhaps light centuries, from the astronomical position of the Earth! It's impossible!"

"And yet we can see it ahead of us," Abna said, amazement in his voice. "Earth is no longer where it used to be—a member of a system with a G-type dwarf for a sun. That is the Earth ahead of us, mysteriously transported to this Milky Way Galaxy."

There was a long silence as the incredible fact was digested. Earth apparently had wandered light centuries from its normal place and was now a solitary planet in the midst of the Galaxy ahead.

The Amazon suddenly made up her mind and went to the control panel, increasing the *Ultra*'s speed.

"Whatever else needs investigating, this certainly does!" she exclaimed. "There seems no conceivable explanation for such a happening. Worlds just don't wander around space and cover light centuries of distance without a very good reason."

The others were silent, yet agreeing with her, staring at the small green point in the stars ahead, toward which they were hurtling with ever-mounting velocity.

ABOUT THE AUTHOR

British writer **JOHN RUSSELL FEARN** was born near Manchester, England, in 1908. As a child he devoured the science fiction of Wells and Verne, and was a voracious reader of the Boys' Story Papers. He was also fascinated by the cinema, and first broke into print in 1931 with a series of articles in *Film Weekly*.

He then quickly sold his first novel, *The Intelligence Gigantic*, to the American magazine, *Amazing Stories*. Over the next fifteen years, writing under several pseudonyms, Fearn became one of the most prolific contributors to all of the leading US science fiction pulps, including such legendary publications as *Astounding Stories*, *Startling Stories*, *Thrilling Wonder Stories*, and *Weird Tales*.

During the late 1940s he diversified into writing novels for the UK market, and also created his famous superwoman character, The Golden Amazon, for the prestigious Canadian magazine, the Toronto *Star Weekly*. In the early 1950s in the UK, his fifty-two novels as "Vargo Statten" were bestsellers, most notably his novelization of the film, *Creature from the Black Lagoon*.

Apart from science fiction, he had equal success with westerns, romances, and detective fiction, writing an amazing total of 180 novels—most of them in a period of just ten years—before his early death in 1960. His work has been translated into nine languages, and continues to be reprinted and read worldwide.